M000188554

Carol

Joyce Bennett-Hall

Published by

Copyright © 2019 Joyce Bennett-Hall

All rights reserved.

ISBN: 0-578-55587-5
ISBN-13: 978-0-578-55587-4

Dedication

This book is dedicated to my Mastermind partners:
Nicki Coble, Martha Mutz, and Angela Overby.

To my prayer partners:
Kathryn Hack, Rebekah Kemmerer, and Rev. Sharron Kelly.

To Linda Rhoho, who fielded the story for me.

To Dr. James Mellon, who inspired me to stretch beyond my
reach.

To Shawn Hall, for the many gifts he has given me.

CHAPTER 1

Behind the Scene

"Girl, this isn't my coat. What's wrong with you? Are you dumb?" he asked.

Before Carol could answer she heard, "Marriage is the number one cause of divorce" followed by a roar of laughter. A comedian was doing his routine at the club and it was spilling over into the lobby.

"Are you deaf? Did you hear me? This is not my coat," the man said once more.

Again, a voice from the other room could be heard saying, "I married Miss Right. I just didn't know her first name was always." Another roar of laughter filled the air.

When the laughter died down Carol said, "Sorry sir, but you didn't have your stub. You know, the one I gave you when you came in. If you had kept it, I wouldn't have to be looking through all the gray tweed coats we have."

Just then, Manny, the owner of the club approached the

1

coat room. "What's the problem here, Carol?" Manny asked. Before Carol could answer, the man harshly said, "This girl gave me the wrong coat."

Manny quickly answered and said, "Sir, show me your check stub and we can quickly resolve this problem."
In the background, the comedian was wrapping up and could be heard saying, "All men make mistakes but married men find out about them sooner." Laughter, then thunderous applause followed.

"Hey, this guy is funny", Manny said, then turned back to the man who had been giving Carol a hard time and asked a second time, "Now sir can I see your check stub?"

"I can't find my stub. It's probably somewhere on the floor in the other room, but I told her what the coat looked like. A grey tweed with a black under collar and this is what she brought me. Do you see a black under collar?" the man answered with a sarcastic question.

"No," Manny said, "but I see a jerk standing in front of me. Now, one more harsh or rude word to this young lady, I will have Johnny escort you outside, in the cold without any coat." Then added, "Do you understand what I mean?"

Johnny is Manny's right hand. He is a big guy with big guns on his arms and other places on his body. His family owns a restaurant on the Southside of Chicago, a favorite hangout for the Chicago Outfit, otherwise known as the Chicago mob. His father is one of the kingpins in the Outfit running different rackets and loan sharking. Johnny did not involve himself in his dad's business and until Manny offered him a job, he could be found hustling in pool halls. Johnny is well known at Behind the Scene and patrons give him the utmost respect for obvious reasons.

Upon hearing that Johnny could be escorting him outside in a very unfriendly manner, the man asked Carol to look one more time for his coat, and this time added, please. She did and found the right one. The man thanked her properly, took his coat and left quickly before Manny changed his mind.

Manny is the owner of Behind the Scene, a nightclub on the Northside of Chicago. His club was a former speakeasy, however, since prohibition ended, he runs a legitimate business, well sort of. Manny runs numbers from the back of his place. The numbers racket, as it is called, is a form of illegal gambling or illegal lottery. The bettor attempts to pick three numbers that would be randomly drawn the next day. The numbers correspond to the last three digits of the number of bets placed by race track bettors on race day at a major race track. Gamblers place their bet with a bookmaker ("bookie"), runners carry the money and betting slips between the betting parlor and the headquarters, which is called a numbers bank. It is quite a racket and very lucrative for the establishment, which is usually a tavern or club of some sort.

Manny met Johnny in a pool hall and actually was hustled by him. Johnny impressed him with his ability to work a room handling anything or anyone that came up against him. The ease in which he worked with people is what prompted Manny to offer Johnny a job. It was a bonus when he found out who Johnny's father was, for he knew his club would be protected from being taken over. Over the past year, several clubs had been infiltrated by some of the Outfit and ultimately were taken over.

Carol is a fun, light-hearted girl, slender but-well-endowed. She wears her long reddish hair pinned up on the sides, allowing loose waves to cascade down in back ending just below her shoulders. High cheekbones and darker skin color from her Native American heritage, and the red hair and green eyes from her Irish heritage complete a beautiful package that stands 5' 1" tall.

Carol works part-time as a hat-check girl, mainly to get out of the house. She is living with her mom and her mom's husband, John. However, it is a big house and John has rented out all the bedrooms except for his and her mom's. She is sleeping in the sunroom, which is part of the parlor and there are all kinds of male boarders wandering around. She has no real privacy and is always worried about giving one of the boarders an unwanted peep show. She has had her bout with horny men, two of them being her uncles.

She is just shy of 18 years old therefore she was worried when she approached Manny, who was a friend of a friend of hers, about a job. He did agree to give her a job as a favor to her friend, however, he made her promise not to go into the club until her birthday. The legal drinking age is 18 years old and Manny did not want to get busted, especially since his club is not entirely on the up and up.

School wasn't for Carol, she wanted to get out into the world and be part of the action. She had felt so suppressed at the Catholic boarding school, although she loved the nuns who took care of her. They were the family she felt she didn't have. Through her childhood experiences, which included her parents bootlegging, her dad's prostitution business, divorce, her sister's disinterest in her, she decided all she really wants in life is a family. A family to make her feel loved, safe and secure. She envied those around her who had that family, her dream. Even though she was living with her mom now, John wasn't warm or even kind and really paid little or no attention to her or her mom. He was more interested in his politics and the income from the boarders in his home.

"Thanks, Manny for sticking up for me. That man is a pill. He always gives me a hard time when he comes in," Carol said.

"We stick up for our own here, and you are part of our family. It's nice to have a young filly around. Keeps the rest of us on our toes."

"So now I'm a horse?" Carol said chuckling.

"Yes, and a frisky one," Manny responded.

With that, a couple came up holding stubs in their hands. Carol turned around to find the appropriate coats. Manny shook the man's hand and went back into the club. The couple thanked Carol for their coats, put money in the tip jar, and said, as they were leaving, "Have a good night." Although she had only been working at Behind the Scene for a short time, she knew she was in the right place, for she felt alive for the first time in a very long time.

CHAPTER 2

Pass Me a Banana, Please!

"Happy Birthday to you, Happy Birthday to you, Happy Birthday dear Carol, Happy Birthday to you." The band did a drum roll and everybody yelled out, "Speech, speech."

Carol was beaming with joy. This was her 18th birthday and Manny had arranged for the band to come in early, just before the club opened to the public. The club was filled with the waitresses, waiters, busboys, bartenders, floor girl, Johnny, and Manny.

A cake with white frosting, red roses, and Happy Birthday Carol written in red across the top sat on one of the tables next to a package wrapped in a big red bow. A gold vase filled with long stem red roses sat on a smaller table in front. Manny knew that Carol's favorite color was red and he wanted to be the first man in her life to give her roses...and he was.

"Oh, those roses and that cake are so beautiful. Thanks to all of you for making my birthday so special. Manny thank you for my very first alcoholic drink, well, my first legal alcoholic drink. What do you call this again, a pink something?" Carol asked.

"It's a Pink Lady. It's the "in" drink of all the high societal ladies. I thought I would start you out right."

With that, everyone raised their glasses and toasted Carol. She was beaming with joy. She thought, this just may be my new family as she took the last swallow of her drink.

"Open up your present honey," one of the waitresses said.

With that, Johnny handed her the package with the big red bow. Carol slowly opened it and when she saw what was inside, she gasped. "Oh, I have never had anything so beautiful. I adore it." It was a lovely pale blue angora sweater. Each short puffy sleeve had two pearl buttons that matched pearl buttons on the collar.

While Carol was holding up her sweater and feeling its softness, one of the waitresses lit the 18 candles on top of the cake and said, "Carol, it's time to make your wish. Make it a good one honey and blow out the candles."

Carol closed her eyes, wished with all her might, opened her eyes, puckered up her lips and blew. All the candles went out, and everyone clapped. Someone handed her a knife and she made the first cut. She knew as she withdrew the knife her wish would come true.....someday she would have her very own family, for she wanted that more than anything else in the world.

"I hate to break up this party but we got us a special performer tonight. A dame that sings wearing a fruit bowl on her head. She is the new rage around town and has made the circuit of all the high-end clubs. So, we need to be on our toes, for the place is going to be packed. Carol, do you think you could handle the floor?"

"Do I? Yes! Oh, I don't have a uniform," Carol responded quickly.

Faye, one of the waitresses, jumped into the conversation with, "That's all right, there are some extras in the back room. Come on, let's see if any of them fit you. You will do great and look as pretty as a picture."

Faye ushered her to a room at the back of the club next to where the bookie was taking bets. Remnants of the birthday celebration were quickly being put away and each member of the band was cleaning or tuning their instruments. Johnny was helping the bartender set up for the night and waitresses were checking the tables for the appropriate setups and accoutrements.

Dark paneling covered the walls and mirrors had been strategically placed with electrical lighting that gave the appearance of flickering candles. During performances when the house lights were turned off these remained on, creating a romantic glow or radiance as the room seemed to be engulfed in candlelight.

Behind the Scene could accommodate over 600 patrons and every table was covered by a white linen tablecloth and a silver vase that held one flower. Each chair was upholstered in a light-colored grey material matching the darker grey carpet. A shiny gold rail separated the tables that were raised in the back part of the room from the ones closer to the stage.

Carol stepped out of the back wearing a cute black lacy skirt with a red top with gold double breasted buttons down the front and a red pillbox hat on her head.

She walked into the club and Johnny whistled then turned to Manny and said, "She's quite the looker."

She felt like a "looker" and was excited to be part of this big evening. "Thank you, I am ready to go," Carol said excitedly.

Faye entered the room with a box like tray filled with cigarettes, cigars, candy, and some trinkets. "Here honey, let me show you how to carry this," Faye said.

Once Carol got the box tray on right, she was surprised that it wasn't really all that heavy. Now for sure, she was ready to go. She didn't have long to wait, for Manny came into the room and gave his nightly instructions to everyone for the evening. Afterward when everyone took their assigned places, Johnny opened the doors.

As people walked through the doors they were greeted by several hostesses and then ushered to different tables. Carol had always been in the coat room and didn't get a chance to see all of the activity that took place seating guests. It was quite exciting and looked like it was a well-orchestrated dance. Guests were seated, bus boys bringing water, barmaids approaching, while the band was playing dinner music in the background, with no one missing a step. It was all very exciting to Carol and she couldn't wait to get into the dance.

Manny instructed her to walk through the tables in the back first and not to approach until people had their drinks. He felt when people are drinking, they are more likely to want to have a cigarette or even buy something for their wife or girlfriend. At first, she was a little shy about asking, however, after the first table asked for a pack of cigarettes, she loosened up and started approaching tables. After a while she even started to respond and interact with the guests, letting out her bubbly personality.

Carol was having a great time walking around and talking with people and many of them even bought some of the trinkets, plus gave her extra money as well. Tips, she was making tips, much more than what she was getting as a hat check girl. Things were going great until she tripped over a man's foot and went sprawling into the next table. Somehow, she managed to hang onto her tray, but her hat was now on the side of her head and one of her shoes was nowhere to be found.

To make matters worse the house lights went off, a voice roared through the crowd announcing the nights' entertainer. With that, a lady with lots of beads around her neck, dressed in multiple layers of bright color clothing started to sing. *Manny was right, she does have a fruit bowl on her head*, Carol thought.

The gentleman who she was sprawled out in front of helped her get up. She straightened her hat and hobbled off to the side of the room. It was too dark to find her other shoe now. Fruit basket lady was singing and dancing and the crowd seemed to really like her, for everyone was swaying to the music and some were even clapping. *Boy, the house is really packed tonight, I hope my shoe doesn't get stepped on and ruined*, Carol thought worriedly.

Carol stood leaning against a wall for the whole first set. As soon as the singer left the stage and the lights came back on, she started scanning the room for her shoe. She saw a very handsome man walking toward her and he was carrying her shoe.

"I believe this is yours," said Mr. Handsome.

"Oh, thank you so much. I feel like Cinderella," Carol replied.

"You are quite welcome, Cinderella. It was my pleasure to return your shoe. Shall we see if it fits?"

"It does," Carol laughed.

"Again, it was my pleasure to return your shoe. My name is Eddie and I hope you come by my table," and then he went back to where he had been sitting – alone.

Eddie is in the Navy reserves and just came back from a two-week stint up North and was to meet some of his buddies here at the club. His buddies never showed, however, he decided to have a drink or two and watch the show.

Eddie comes from a well-to-do family on the South Side of Chicago, well-educated and graduated in the top of his class.

Some would say he is a "wheeler-dealer" as he is always coming up with one scheme or another to make money.

He enlisted in the Navy reserve right after graduation because he wanted to travel the world. He believed all those recruiting propaganda signs but so far the only place he has been is Great Lakes Naval Base north of Chicago. This was his first weekend home in three weeks and he intended to make the most of it.

Carol got her shoe back on, went to the ladies' room, fixed her hat, freshened her face and went back out onto the floor with her box tray.

The first table she went by was Eddie's, saying, "Cigars, cigarettes, candy...."

Eddie interrupted her, "Yes, Cinderella, I would like some cigarettes, please."

Carol handed him the small pack that held four cigarettes and thanked him again for finding her shoe. They talked for a little while until he finally asked her if she would like to get together with him the next day for some fun. Her heart skipped a beat. Even though she felt like jumping up and down, she took in a deep breath and answered calmly.

"Yes, that would be nice. Where would we go to have this fun?" She asked.

He smiled and said, "Outside. We will be having fun outside. Just dress warm and prepare yourself to have the time of your life."

"Okay, will do. Thanks again. I'm looking forward to tomorrow but now I have to get back to work."

As she continued wandering around the room with her box tray, she was curious what he meant by having "the time of your life." No matter what, she was ready to have some fun.

When she met Faye at the end of the evening to return

her tray and uniform, she told her about Mr. Handsome. They were both laughing and giggling as they were about to leave the club when Manny stopped them and asked what was so funny. Faye blurted out Carol's news.

"What do you know about him?" Manny asked Carol acting like a protective father.

"Well, he found my shoe and seems really nice," she answered.

"He found your shoe?" Manny asked looking very perplexed.

Carol told him that when she tripped and fell, she lost her shoe. Then went on to tell him the rest of the story.

"I'm sure he's a nice enough fellow. However, I'll ask Johnny to check him out."

"You're worse than Momma," Carol said laughing.

"As I told you earlier, we take care of our own here. By the way, you did a great job tonight."

"Thanks, Manny. I had fun. Thanks again for my birthday celebration."

As she was leaving the club she thought, *today has been the best birthday celebration I have ever had. Who would have thought it included being Cinderella for an evening. I wonder if I just met Prince Charming.*

CHAPTER 3

Catch the Wind in Them Sails

Carol put on her insulated leggings, two sweaters, and two pairs of socks then squeezed her feet into snow boots. It was dead of winter and the temperature had been in the single digits for quite a spell. Eddie had said to dress warm and this was the best she could do, hoping it would be enough. She kissed her mom goodbye and quickly went outside. They had arranged to meet at Behind the Scene as Carol wasn't ready for him to come to her house.

Walking toward the club she spotted a dark blue coupe car parked at the curb. At first, she became apprehensive as Carol knew there had been some mob hits on clubs over the last couple of months and it looked like a car a gangster would drive. She was relieved when she saw Eddie step out of the car.

"Hey Cinderella, over here," he yelled.

"I am coming. I have so much clothing on that it is hard to walk fast," she said laughing.

"You will need it where we are going," he said. He escorted her to the front seat, closed the door, walked around the car and climbed in behind the wheel.

"This your car?" Carol asked.

"Yes, however, my younger brother and I share it. He uses the car when I am gone with the reserves, and sometimes I think he thinks that it is his," Eddie said.

They continued talking as they drove through the city and ended up just past downtown at the rocks along Lake Michigan. Carol looked around and really couldn't figure out where they were going, until, he came around the car, opened her door so she could get out, and as she did, he pointed to a small boat with two sails on it. It didn't really look like a boat, however, since it had sails, she assumed it was.

"Is that a boat?" Carol asked.

"Yep, an ice boat. I built it myself. It really moves on the ice. Have you ever been ice sailing before?"

"No, but it looks dangerous," Carol said a little apprehensively about this whole ice sailing thing.

"It just looks that way, and it can be for someone who has never steered an ice boat before. However, my family and I have been ice sailing a long time, so, I am a seasoned and experienced ice boat captain. Are you ready?" Eddie asked.

"As ready as I will ever be, captain," Carol responded.

They walked to the lake's edge, where Eddie had the boat tied to a small piece of what was left of a dock. When they reached the boat, he helped Carol into the makeshift seat, which was in the middle between what looked like thin pontoon rails. The little boat looked like big T, somewhere between a crossbow and the frame of a small aircraft. She cautiously got situated in the make-shift seat, hoping she wouldn't fall off.

"Well captain, I'm seated and ready to go. Anchors away!"

Eddie responded with a fun salute and yelled, "Here we go."

Standing next to the boat he reached in, pulled a lever, pushed another and the boat moved away from the rocks. Eddie jumped on just in time as the wind caught the sails and the boat took off. It went gliding across the ice smooth as silk. However, the boat was picking up too much speed and Eddie started to zig-zag the boat to slow it down. Even though Eddie was busy moving the sail this way and that to keep the boat upright, he took a moment to look at Carol. She was laughing and squealing with delight. He even heard a happy scream.

Carol had never experienced anything like this. It was exhilarating. The cold air hitting her face caused her eyes to fill with water and tears to roll down her cheeks. Wiping her cheek with her scarf, she said, "I love this." Although Eddie couldn't hear her clearly, he knew she was having a good time by the way she was laughing. She did love it and could feel her adrenaline running high. She was exuberant. They had been sailing for a little over an hour when Eddie started to steer the iceboat back to the rocks. He got it as close as he could so Carol would be able to get out of the boat and step right onto the rocks.

"Well, how did you like that?" Eddie asked.

"I loved it. I felt so alive and free out on the ice. Thank you so much for giving me the "time of my life." Carol answered throwing her arms around his neck and kissing him on his check.

Eddie laughed and said, "I'm glad you liked it, and if this is how you say thank you, I have to come up with more ways to give you "the time of your life." Now, how about getting something to eat?" He asked.

"I would love that," Carol answered. And with that, off the two of them went to a nearby eatery. That was the beginning of a new budding romance.

CHAPTER 4

Thrills, Chills, and Chopsticks

The following several weeks when Carol wasn't at work, she was with Eddie. Manny kept his word and did have Johnny check Eddie out. Since Eddie had made a reservation the night he came in, he had a telephone number. He found out that Eddie's family was very financially well off and had a big home just a little south of downtown. The family was in real estate, both residential as well as commercial. He did find out that Eddie was in the Naval Reserves and he found nothing that would be of concern. When he reported what he found out to Manny, they decided that Eddie was probably an all right stand-up guy. They dropped the subject of Eddie and got about the business of the day.

One of the things that Eddie and Carol liked to do was skate. They spent a couple of nights a week roller skating at a local roller rink. One evening Eddie entered them in a skating dance contest, and they came in second. Carol was so proud of their second-place trophy that she brought it to the club to show Manny.

Late one morning Eddie picked up Carol and drove north of Chicago to a local airport. He was taking Carol to lunch to a restaurant that overlooked the runways. He thought she might like watching the planes take off and land while they were eating.

"Well, here we are," Eddie said.

"I can't wait to see all the activity of the planes," Carol responded.

"Carol, can you wait a little longer for lunch?"

"Sure, why?"

"I have arranged an added surprise to our luncheon date."

With that, he parked the car, came around, opened the door and helped Carol out. He then escorted her across the parking lot to one of the hangars. As they approached the door, a man came out and greeted them.

"Good morning," The man said. "Are you Mr. Walski?"

"Yes, and we have an appointment with you I believe," Eddie responded.

Carol was getting butterflies in her stomach for she had an inkling as to what the surprise might be. And she was right. A plane was rolled out onto the tarmac and Eddie and Carol were ushered around to the side of the small plane.

"This is my surprise," Eddie said. "We are going to take a look-see flight over Chicago."

"Oh, it does sound like fun, is it safe? Carol asked.

The man answered, "Yes, quite. You have the best pilot around, me. My name is Wayne and this here baby is one of the safest planes around, a brand-new Cessna."

Eddie and Carol climbed in. Eddie sat in the front next to the pilot with Carol in the seat behind them. Next thing Carol knew the engine roared, propellers started to revolve, and the plane was moving. All of a sudden, they were in the air. At first, Carol felt scared, then a little queasy, but both things passed when she realized she could see for miles when she looked out the window. How thrilling. The pilot flew the plane over downtown and she could see Michigan Avenue, the shoreline, the Wrigley building, and the museums.

Eddie leaned over to the pilot and he seemed to be directing him toward something. Carol felt the plane make another turn and go down. At first, Carol's heart jumped for she thought something was wrong. However, when the plane leveled off, she realized where they were. They were flying over Behind the Scene. On their way back to the airport, Carol was sorry that her first flying experience was soon coming to an end. They landed and the pilot rolled toward the hangar. When the plane stopped, the pilot got up and helped Carol and Eddie disembark the plane.

Once off, they walked hand and hand toward the restaurant. While she was eating her hamburger and drinking her malt, Carol watched the planes take off and land. She was having such a great time with Eddie and loved all the adventures he took her on.

When May rolled around, Eddie and Carol walked, as usual, hand and hand into Riverview, the world's largest privately-owned amusement park. It was opening day and Carol's first time visiting the park.

Carol's family never had the discretionary money for such frivolity. The day she walked in on her dad and another woman, her world changed. Her dad left and she found herself in a convent-like setting being raised by nuns. She always felt alone and missed her mom and her family so much. She had wished with all her might that they all could get back together. That never happened and she vowed one day she would have a family of her own.

෨෧෯

Laughing on rollercoasters, riding the horses on the Carousel pretending to be riding on the range, eating hot dogs, cotton candy and getting romantic in the Tunnel of Love made their day an unforgettable one. As they were walking out of the park, Carol turned to Eddie, threw her arms around his neck, kissed him on the cheek.

"Thank you for giving me another "time of my life" day!" Carol exclaimed.

"So, you do always say thank you the same way. Boy, I do have my work cut out for me, but I'm going to love this job." Eddie said chuckling.

"Are you too full of cotton candy to get a bite to eat?"

"No, so let's go to get some Chinese. I understand that restaurant on Irving Park is pretty good."

"Sounds great!"

When their dinner came, Carol looked at the chopsticks and gave the "help me" look to Eddie. He picked up the cue and quickly asked the young girl who brought them their dinner for some silverware. Carol let out a relieved sigh, for she wasn't up to learning how to use chopsticks this night, she just wanted to relax after such a busy day.

After dinner, a young girl dressed in a traditional Chinese wrap brought them each a fortune cookie. Carol opened hers and read it out loud, "This is your lucky day." She continued and said, "It sure has been a great day, not sure about lucky. I wasn't very lucky at any of those games we tried today." Then she asked him to open up his cookie and read his fortune.

Eddie broke open his cookie and pulled out the little piece of paper inside. He began reading, "This is your lucky day too."

Carol smiled and said, "What?"

"There's more. It says this is your lucky day too because she is going to say yes."

Carol looking a little perplexed thinking there was some kind of joke happening asked, "Yes to what?"

With that Eddie reached in his pocket and pulled out a ring box, opened it and as he put it before her, he said, "Carol, I'm in love with you, will you marry me?"

At first, Carol could not find her voice, until Eddie said, "Well. say something."

"I...I just didn't expect this." She picked up the box and just stared at the ring. "Oh, it is so beautiful. I have never seen anything so beautiful."

"So, Carol, will you be my wife?" Eddie asked feeling a little apprehensive.

"The fortune cookie already told you the answer. Yes, of course, I'll marry you. I would love to marry you and be Mrs. Eddie Walski."

She got up, walked over to Eddie's chair, put her arms around his neck, bent down and kissed him lovingly on his lips. He stood up and reciprocated by putting his arms around her and engaged in a long passionate kiss. Afterward, Eddie took the ring out of the box and slipped it on Carol's finger. She kissed him again.

"Let's go get a drink and celebrate," Eddie suggested.

As they were preparing to leave, people started clapping

and several of them actually stood up from their chairs. One couple actually came over to congratulate them. Loud clapping and a standing ovation in a Chinese restaurant is not something that one sees every day.

CHAPTER 5

Dreams Come True?

Carol and Eddie had a small intimate wedding ceremony in a Catholic church followed by a gathering at his parent's home. Carol's sister Ruth came with her husband William and son Danny. John and her mom came along with Serena, her mom's best friend. Manny, Johnny and Faye came from the club. Carol was so happy because her birthday wish had come true. She now had the beginning of a family of her own, though there was one thing in the back of her mind that was bothering her. Lately Eddie was drinking more than usual.

The evening she became engaged he drank, she thought, more than usual. She had shrugged it off because it was a celebratory evening. Today, he was drinking heavily again. Carol once again shrugged it off as it was another day of celebration and scolded herself for being such a prude.

Eddie found a beautiful big apartment on the Southside of Chicago, just beyond downtown. The parlor's sunroom had a bow window overlooking the street. A formal dining room was next to the parlor, with a doorway to the kitchen, which also had a bay window that jetted out for a table and chairs. Cream colored cabinets surrounded the four-leg stove and built-in refrigerator. It also had a fold-down ironing board tucked away within the cabinets. Since Carol still worked at Behind the Scene, she would be able to get there easily as the bus stop was right across the street from the apartment.

Eddie's family furnished the apartment for them, including furniture for a baby's room. Money was no object for them which was so unfamiliar to Carol. At first, she felt uncomfortable about receiving so much from them. However, his family was so kind and loving that they assured her that it was their pleasure to help. Once she got comfortable with everything, she settled in with ease. She loved her new life!

Eddie was involved with guys who always had new ways to make money, usually illegally. One of the guys had access to stolen goods, mostly jewelry, which Eddie would market. Eddie was involved with other rackets as well, like loan sharking, which is lending money and charging unreasonable amounts of interest. People who got in over their heads owing gambling debts were prime customers for loan sharking.

Carol always wondered where he got his money, but never asked. She didn't want to rock the boat and cause any trouble that could end her dream of having a family. Carol liked being taken care of or looked after and knew too many questions or probing into Eddie's business life could end her dream.

Carol believed if a woman lets a man think she is dependent on him, then the man feels more like a man and will provide for her and that was very important to Carol. Eddie did provide and take care of her in all the ways that were important to Carol. In reality, Carol was becoming her own woman and in the not so far future, she would have to rely on her resources.

Carol loved her apartment and enjoyed creating a home for her and Eddie. Life was good for the couple, and when Carol didn't think things could get any better, she became pregnant. Carol thought she might be pregnant since she missed her two months of her monthly cycle. However, she has been waiting to hear from the doctor the results of the testing. Today, she got the call that her tests came back positive, she was going to have a baby!

She was in seventh heaven and was dancing around the apartment singing "I'm going to have a baby, I'm going to have a baby, I'm going to have a baby" to the tune of one of the songs that fruit head lady sang at the club. She even put a little cha cha cha in her step as she sang. When the doorbell rang, it startled Carol and interrupted her happy dance. She stopped singing and went to the door. When she opened it, she was surprised and delighted to see Faye. "Hi, oh I am so glad to see you, come in."

❧∽⑤

Faye is a waitress at Behind the Scene and is Carol's best friend. Carol felt so fortunate to have Faye in her life, for she is the first real friend Carol has had. Faye is a couple of years older than Carol and recently was, as she would say, "dumped by her fiancé for another woman" and meeting Carol, who made everyone feel better about themselves, had lifted her spirits. Faye has her own apartment in the city and is a transplant from Nebraska where she grew up on a farm. Being bored with milking cows she set off for the big city.

Faye met Sam at a restaurant where she was working and she thought it was love at first sight for both of them. Sam was a rover and a womanizer and love at first site was not in his DNA. When he got bored with the waitress from the country, he moved on to a more sophisticated woman and it didn't hurt that she was an older wealthy woman.

⁂

"Carol I just heard about your good news and wanted to come over and give you a hug and congratulate you. I am so happy for you, for I know how important this is for you." Faye said hugging Carol.

"Thank you, but how did you know? I haven't even told Eddie yet. I just found out today." Carol responded.

"Manny knew you were going to the doctor today and let's just say, he has his ways to know things. Anyway, again, I am so happy for you and Eddie."

So much for privacy between doctor and patient, Carol thought. "I am so glad you came by, I was just bursting at the seams to tell someone and Eddie won't be home until later."

"I just stopped by for a minute. I have to get going for I am working tonight and it is the opening night for that yummy looking singer. The house will be packed. Be glad you won't be there tonight."

"Yes, I am glad. I want to tell Eddie the good news. He will be so happy. I am working tomorrow night so I will see you then. Thanks so much for stopping by! Since Manny has his ways of knowing things, ask him what am I having, a boy or a girl," she laughed and hugged Faye good-bye.

"I don't think I'll ask him, I'll save that question for you. Love you, bye," Faye said giggling as she left the apartment.

As Carol waved good-bye and shut the door, she wondered if Eddie would really be happy about the baby. She started to have worry thoughts. *Eddie likes to party and do exciting things and I won't be able to do some of those things for a while. Then when the baby comes, partying as much as we do may have to stop, or at least calm down a bit. We probably won't be able to do as many of the things Eddie likes to do. Oh, I hope this baby won't be an obstacle to our happiness together.* She put those thoughts out of her mind and reassured herself that he would be just as excited as she is.

Carol's news of her pregnancy was received with excitement from Eddie. When Carol told him, he was going to be a father he picked her up and swung her around in the air and then he started dancing with her. Carol scolded herself for worrying if Eddie would be happy with the news of them having a baby.

Eddie was beaming and said, "We are going to have a little Carol, I know it!"

"Or a little Eddie," Carol added. They both started to laugh. Carol's dream of a family seems to becoming a reality.

CHAPTER 6

A Middleweight Champion "A Winner"

Eddie and Carol continued enjoying their time together and spending more quiet times at home when Carol wasn't working. Eddie was still wheeling and dealing and Carol still did not ask what he did although she did wonder why he would work such odd hours. Many a night she could tell that Eddie had been drinking a bit too much. Eddie continued his once a month mandatory reserve weekend and she just figured that a lot of drinking went on at night on those weekends. Men were being drafted for the war and she was sure that the men were worried about being activated...and so was Carol. So once again, she shrugged off Eddie's drinking. Deep down she worried about Eddie's increased drinking and this time she did not scold herself for she knew that this was a potential threat to her dream.

Just before the baby was due, Eddie was called for a

special reserve weekend. He was gone when Carol went into labor and Faye took his place. Faye took Carol to Saint Xavier hospital where she began her many hours of labor. When Carol complained about the pain, one of the nuns, told her that she had had her fun, now she was paying the price for that fun.

Carol felt afraid and so alone. She wasn't used to the harshness of nuns, for they were always very loving to her in the boarding school. She knew that some nuns viewed procreation as the only reason to have intercourse, not for pleasure. She thought, why are these nuns treating me with hostility? I am having a baby for god sakes. This experience colored Carol's opinion about having another child. That color was fear, for her labor was long and hard.

Faye overheard the remark and immediately reported the nun to the head of obstetrics. That seemed to make things worse for Carol and Faye felt guilty for reporting the nun. Another nurse finally did take over. She informed Faye that the nurse she had complained about worked at an orphanage and sometimes she does get surly because she sees so many babies coming into the world just to be given up. Carol's baby must have known something was up and decided to finally push its way out.

"Mrs. Walski, you have a beautiful baby girl...and I can tell she is going to be a winner. Oh yes, she's a winner," the doctor said.

Even though Carol was drained from the long labor and hard delivery, she asked if she could hold her daughter. She looked down at the tiny bundle that the nurse laid next to her, pulled back the top of the blanket and said, "I love you. You are so precious. Welcome, Ann Elizabeth Walski."

With the words barely out of her mouth, the nurse picked up Ann Elizabeth and said, "You get your rest now. I'll bring your baby back as soon as we clean her up and take all her vitals."

Carol was beat and even though she wanted Ann to stay, she felt a sense of exhaustion come over her. She closed her eyes and fell fast asleep.

⌒∾⌒

Carol and Ann Elizabeth got acquainted over the next few days and Faye had arranged for one of Johnny's friends to pick Carol and Ann up from the hospital. Carol got ready and dressed Ann in her first little outfit. Ann weighed in at 9 lbs. and 4 oz. and was 22 inches long...a middleweight champion. Carol waited and waited and waited. Johnny's friend never came.

Carol was surprised to see Faye show up in the late afternoon.

"Faye, Johnny's friend didn't show up. Although, you know that already or you wouldn't be here. What happened?" Carol asked.

"Oh, honey, let's get you and the baby downstairs and out of this hospital and I will fill you in," Faye responded.

Manny was waiting downstairs with the car. Faye got Carol and Ann situated, and filled her in on the story. Johnny's friend, whose name is Tony, was shot outside his home. Apparently, he was just leaving his house when a car pulled up and a man inside pointed a gun and shot him. There was a witness to the shooting, unfortunately, they did not get a good look at the shooter, and really, it wouldn't have mattered anyway. People were too afraid of the Chicago mob to tell what they saw.

Carol felt sick to her stomach. She felt guilty for his death. If he wasn't on his way to pick her up, he would still be alive. She expressed her feelings out loud and Manny assured her that it was just a matter of time that Tony got his.

"He had been playing two ends against the middle trading and dealing with both the Northside and Southside mobs. Someone ratted him out and he got caught, that's all. That is the name of the game that he was playing," he explained.

Carol's thoughts went to, *how in the hell did I get to be part of this situation. Of course, when you come from a family that has bootlegged and your father is a pimp and god knows what else, and I'm friends with a mobster's son, working at a club where there is illegal gambling, of course, I would be in this situation. All I ever wanted was a family of my own, well I certainly have one, don't I? A crime family and a husband who probably is involved with things just as shady.*

"Carol, are you alright?" Faye asked.

"Yes, just tired," Carol responded. "I'll be better once I get home and rest a little."

Manny took Carol home and Faye helped her inside with Ann. When they left, Carol went to the kitchen, poured herself a glass of water and sighed. She was glad to be home. Carol put Ann in her bassinet, pulled it next to the couch where she was about to lay down but was interrupted by the door opening. It was Eddie.

"What? How did you get to come home early from the base? However, you did it, I am so glad you are home." Carol said.

Eddie walked over to the couch, bent down, kissed Carol and said, "So am I. I told them that you were getting ready to deliver our baby so, they did give me a pass to leave early, but I couldn't get a ride any faster. So sorry, I wasn't there." Eddie then looked down on Ann sleeping and said, "Oh she is beautiful, looks just like her mommy."

"Thanks, honey. The doctor who delivered Ann said he could tell that she was a winner."

"Yes, she is and so are you. But I am the real winner for I

have won the jackpot, a beautiful amazing wife and a precious daughter."

Carol thought, *and now I have my family, my real family, a family I can call my own.*

Carol filled Eddie in on her experience in the hospital and what happened to Johnny's friend Tony. He listened attentively and then leaned forward and lifted Carol off the couch, hugged her and said, "I'm so sorry I wasn't there for you. I'm here now. I love you so very much and I am so sorry that I haven't been around very much recently. However, that is going to change, starting now."

Eddie put his things away and told Carol to stay resting and he would make them something to eat, an "Eddie special". Pouring himself a drink, he vowed to himself to be a better husband from this day forward. A flickering thought flashed through his mind which gave him a start, am I really ready to be a husband...and now a father? He quickly dismissed the thought and started his "Eddie special."

CHAPTER 7

Hey Buddy, Need a Loan?

Eddie felt like he was in a vice. One of the reasons he fell in love with Carol was her verve for life and her openness of character. Ever since Ann joined them Carol isn't willing to do the things that she did before. She has a lot of fear of getting hurt and not being able to take care of Ann. Well, at least that is what she says. The truth of the matter is she doesn't want to leave Ann.

Carol is completely consumed with Ann. It's like Ann filled a giant hole in her. Every time he planned something for them to do as a couple, she had an excuse for not wanting to go. He was starting to get itchy feet and cabin fever.

Carol was no longer working for Manny. Eddie was making enough money to take care of things. He also felt pressure from the work that he does. Eddie works for a group of people who do "salary lending" otherwise known as loansharking. The prospective borrower of money would be investigated by one or several of the group to determine if the man had a steady job and how reliable it was. The borrower would sign many complicated forms virtually saying that he was borrowing on his future salary. In the event that the borrower failed to meet the payments, the collection was attempted by threatening to inform the employer of the debt or by harassment of various sorts.

Eddie picked up the payments and was the messenger of threats and harassment. It was starting to get to him. The last guy he tried to collect from pulled a gun on him. It was obvious he objected to being threatened.

Eddie was worried about the Chicago Outfit, the mob, retaliating against his bosses for hanging a shingle out for "Salary Lending." So far, the Outfit only did loansharking on the Southside. Lately, they have been moving in on other businesses close to the Northside.

The offices of the group that he worked with were on the near Northside and that worried him along with borrowers pulling guns on him.

Eddie has been a "wheeler-dealer" since he was a kid growing up in an affluent household. In school, he bought things that were not available to most of the kids in his school and upsold them. The things included watches, cuff links, tie clips and sometimes articles of clothing. In some of the restaurants he frequented he would offer his watch as collateral until he had the money to pay the check. A homespun credit system. He really was ahead of his time.

Eddie thought by joining the Naval Reserves he would beat the draft. Going one weekend a month and two weeks a year wouldn't be so bad. However, it now looks like his unit may be activated and sent to sea. This just squeezed the vice, he felt like he was in, just a bit tighter. The vice loosened a little when he found out that married men with a family were the last to be deployed. That gave him a little breathing room.

Eddie was worried about one more thing. When Carol told him about Johnny's friend, Tony, being shot outside his house, he got a sharp stabbing feeling inside his gut. He had hidden his reaction from Carol, for he knew he would have to get into a long explanation as to why he was reacting to the news in that way. Tony was also one of the guys that collected payments for the group he worked with. He knew Tony and he also knew he was not part of the mob and that worried him. *So, who shot him? Maybe, someone, he collected payment from or someone he had been harassing for payment.*

He had to see a client today to pick up a payment and he was really apprehensive. Eddie drove to the client's home as he has done several times before. Today was a regular scheduled pick-up. He drove up to the curb, parked and cautiously walked up the two steps and used the door knocker to announce his arrival. The door opened and the borrower stood in the doorway looking like he hadn't slept in days.

"I'm here to pick up the scheduled payment," Eddie said.

"I don't have it this month," the man replied. He went on to say that his wife had become ill, had been in the hospital and just recently came home. He has been taking care of his wife and had not worked for a week.

Eddie just stood there and couldn't bring himself to harass this man. Instead, he offered to see if the group would give him a pass for this month. The man was grateful and assured him that he would have the payment next month. Eddie said good-by, walked back to his car, got in, and drove away feeling relieved. He drove to the offices of his employer.

Eddie was all revved up when he parked the car in front of the offices of The Lending Firm that had "If you have too much month at the end of your money, we can help you" written under the name. He thought it should read, *we take all your money and harass and threaten you until you give it back.*

He walked in and headed towards the inner office when the girl at the front desk, who happened to be on the phone, covered the mouthpiece and said, "Sorry Mr. Walski, Mr. Sullivan has a client with him."

Eddie turned around, nodded a thank you to her and then took a chair. He decided to wait for Bill Sullivan. He wanted to quit while he was charged up to do so.

A few minutes later, the door opened and a short meek looking man walked out and Bill Sullivan walked behind him, shook his hand and said, "Good doing business with you. The Lending Firm has your back."

Eddie thought, *what he really means short meek man, The Lending Firm will stab you in the back.* As that thought was leaving, Don motioned for him to come into his office.

"Well, Eddie, what brings you in today? You're not scheduled until tomorrow," Bill Sullivan asked.

"Two things. First the client I saw today, I want to ask you to give him a pass until next month. His wife has been sick and he hasn't worked for a while-" Eddie was interrupted by Bill Sullivan, "We don't give anyone a pass. How could we stay in business if we did?"

"I just thought this one time we could. The guy has made every payment on time. It wouldn't hurt. He may end up being a repeat customer if you give him a break."

"Well, I see what you mean. Okay, on your say so, just this once. Now, what was the second reason you came in to see me?"

"As you know Carol and I now have a little girl and things have changed for me. Being out as many evenings as I have been is causing me some concerns. I am already gone one weekend a month and as it is, we don't have that much alone time anymore. Babies make it their business to see to that. So, for that reason, I think I need to leave the firm."

"Well, if it is time you want, I'll make sure that you get the clients that you can visit during the day. That is easily solved."

"There is another reason as well. Tony, who was one of us was shot and killed and since I don't think he was part of the Outfit, I worry that one of the clients he was harassing killed him. One of my clients pulled a gun on me."

Bill looked around the room, walked to the door, opened it, looked around the lobby, shut it and then returned to his chair.

"We took care of Tony," Bill said.

"What?" Eddie shouted.

"Eddie, we found out that he was pocketing some of the pick-ups and covered it by changing the numbers on the original contracts. He was stealing from us."

"So you killed him?"

"No, don't be stupid. We had him killed. Stealing from the firm is capital punishment and everyone has been told that when they joined this family."

"We're not the mob for God sakes. Capital punishment? Who set you up as judge and jury?"

"Me. It is my firm and I can run it the way I want."

"Well, I want no part of it, I am quitting!"

"Things don't work that way. You signed up for this job and you're stuck with it. You don't get to leave. We're family, get it? You stay and nothing happens to Carol and Ann. I'll see to it that you only have to collect from daytime clients."

Eddie left slamming the door behind him so hard that the vibration cracked the front window. He had to decide whether or not to tell Carol. He decided to wait and tell her later. In the meantime, he would go about his business collecting and harassing clients until he could figure things out, and that is exactly what he did.

CAROL

CHAPTER 8

Take Off My Robe You Hussy!

Ann's Christening was held at Eddie's parent's home and it was quite a shindig. Carol's mom, John, Ruth, William, Danny and Manny, and Johnny from the club were all there to celebrate Ann. Eddies' parents invited their extended family members along with neighbors to join them in celebrating their granddaughter as well as show her off.

Eddie was drinking heavily and became inappropriate by arguing loudly over some political decisions that the government had made. Carol was embarrassed, so she asked Eddie to check on Ann who was sleeping upstairs. She was hoping to interrupt the debate and it worked. Eddie agreed and left the room to check on Ann and he did not return to the party. After everyone had left, Carol found him sleeping with Ann. Eddie had apparently been rocking Ann to sleep and dozed off himself. Carol thought how sweet they both looked together. She loved both of them so much, her family.

Carol spent her days with Ann. She took her for walks and sometimes Faye would come over and bring lunch. Carol loved spending time with Faye. She would bring Carol the latest gossip from the club and talk about all the performers who were appearing there. Carol missed all that, however, Ann and Eddie were her life now. One day when Faye was visiting, Carol asked if the police ever found out who shot Johnny's friend. Faye said the police just contributed the incident to just one more mobster caught up in something. She never found out that her husband worked with Tony and that their boss had him killed.

Eddie was going about his days collecting payments and was grateful that everyone he had visited lately had the money. Late one afternoon he was making his last pick-up. It was a new client for him. When he knocked on the door a very petite woman in her 20's answered. She was small like Carol, with beautiful wavy blonde hair that hung just below her shoulders.

"Are you Peggy Johnson?" He asked.

"Yes," she answered.

"I'm here to pick up your payment."

"I don't have the money for the payment," Peggy said as she started to cry.

Even though Eddie was not supposed to get personal with a client, he felt the need to ask her what happened because she had burst into tears. He had never had a client do that before. She backed up and started to cry again. She turned and walked into the kitchen and got herself a glass of water. Eddie followed her inside. She sat down at the kitchen table and Eddie pulled up a chair and sat across from her.

Peggy proceeded to tell him that she had just been laid off from her job as a bookkeeper from one of the top restaurants downtown. She went on to admit that she lied to get the job and really couldn't keep up with all the work and do it correctly. She lied because she really needed a job.

Eddie listened and listened and listened, for she continued telling him her life's story. He found himself getting drawn into her. As Peggy continued talking, she leaned towards him and he felt even a stronger pull towards her. He wasn't thinking at this point. He was only feeling. He was feeling what his body was saying and shouldn't have listened. But his body was talking very loudly at this point and if it could have been heard, it would have been a shrill scream.

She reached over and touched his hand and said, "Thank you for listening to me. I live alone and sometimes I get so lonely and yearn to talk to someone about all the things I have shared with you."

Instead of responding to Peggy, he responded to what his body was saying. He leaned across the table and kissed her...and that is how their affair started. Needless to say, he didn't get the payment from her, but he felt she had paid him in a much bigger and better way. So much so, that he delivered her payment to Bill Sullivan using his own money. Eddie delivered that payment for her with a huge smile on his face.

Eddie would see Peggy once a week and continued to make her payments for her. He wasn't in love with her, but the clandestine affair was exciting to him. She was scratching his itch. To him, it really wasn't a meaningful relationship...just a fling. However, she had other ideas. Unbeknownst to Eddie, there were days she would follow him until one day she found out where he lived.

It was true that Carol was consumed with Ann. She loved her so much and spent most of her day playing with her. It was like she was giving Ann all the love and attention that she felt she never got. She gave Eddie that same kind of attention and love for she was so grateful to have a family, a lovely apartment and plenty of food for their table. Carol was so happy and content for she now had a family of her own.

It had been several weeks since that shocking meeting that Eddie had with Bill at The Lending Firm and he felt it was time to tell Carol. So, that night when he got home, he asked Carol to sit and talk with him before she put the dinner on the table. Carol went immediately into fear for she was expecting to hear that his reserve unit was being activated and he was going to be sent out to sea.

"Eddie, what is it, you seem so distressed?" Carol asked.

"I am. I know who shot and killed Johnny's friend Tony." Eddie responded.

"What? How would you know that?"

"I knew Tony. He did the same work I do. You never asked me what I do and I appreciate that. It's time for you to know what I do to earn our money. I work for a group that lends money to people and then harasses or threatens them if they can't pay. This group charges a huge fee and adds that to the loan every month until it is paid."

"Do you threaten people? Did Tony threaten people? Did one of those people shoot Tony?" Carol asked as she got up off the sofa. She was relieved that the news had nothing to do with Eddie being deployed but shocked by what she was hearing. She felt nauseous.

"Yes, I mean no," Eddie said. Then went on to say, "I pick up payments from the people who borrowed money. The only threat we're authorized to make is to tell their employer about the loan, that's all. No strong-arm tactics," Eddie said trying to calm Carol down.

"So, how do you know who shot Tony?" Carol asked sitting back down.

"I went to the owner of the business to quit. I had several

reasons for wanting to do so, but when I tried, the owner made it quite clear that I could not leave. He said that I was part of their family and no one leaves the family. He sounded like a mob boss."

"What? What kind of man is he? What did you say? And was Tony part of the family as well?" Ann asked all in one breath.

"Yes, apparently so. To answer your question about what kind of man he is, he went on to say that he had Tony killed. That's what kind of man he is." Eddie answered. Then added, "He said it was because Tony was skimming money from the payments he was picking up, stealing from the business."

"So why did he tell you about Tony if all you wanted to do was quit," Carol asked looking baffled.

"The reason I wanted to quit was one of my clients pulled a gun on me."

"What?" Carol screamed. "What the hell has this world come to? You could have been killed, all for a job. You had better quit that job. I'll go back to the club and work."

"Calm down, I wasn't shot and I can't quit. Now that Bill told me that he had Tony killed he can't let me leave, and if I do, you and Ann could be in danger. So, I'm stuck, at least for a while. Maybe you and Ann should go to your mom's place for a while until I can figure this thing out."

"I don't really want to, but I do think you are right. I'll tell mom that you are going out of town for a couple of days and I don't want to be alone with Ann."

❧

In the meantime, the day that Peggy followed Eddie home, she stayed in the neighborhood for a while and watched the apartment. Today was the day that Eddie was to go "pick up her payment", however, Peggy decided she would go to his apartment and surprise him instead. She planned to watch the apartment until she saw his wife leave with the baby in the stroller then she would surprise him. Can you imagine how happy and surprised she was when she saw Carol leave with the baby and what looked like an overnight bag? *This is my lucky day*, she thought. *There must be trouble in paradise.*

Peggy approached the apartment door and knocked. Eddie opened it and said, "Whoa, what are you doing here?"

"Today is our scheduled appointment, and I thought I would come to you this time," she said. "I saw your wife leave with an overnight bag, trouble?"

"No, she is going to spend some time with her mom," Eddie responded. "Since you're here, come in," he said.

It didn't take them long to get down to business... the business of fornication, a different form of payment. Eddie found today's encounter even more thrilling and exciting and a little dangerous. That thought aroused him even more. It was exciting for sure, and since Carol was at her mom's he was safe, or was he? Peggy continued to "pay" Eddie most of the day and he collected with a smile.

Carol did go to her mom's, however, she dropped off Ann and told her mom she had an errand to run. She went to the club to talk to Manny and Johnny. She was in luck, they were both there even though it was in the middle of the afternoon. Carol asked to speak to both of them privately. Manny escorted her and Johnny into his office, where Carol relayed everything that Eddie told her. They both listened intently darting their eyes back and forth from each other. Manny and Johnny seemed to be reading each other's thoughts as Carol was relating the information. Manny thanked Carol for stopping by and letting them know what happened to Tony.

After she left the office, Manny said, "Johnny, you know what to do, don't you?"

"Yep, I'll talk to my father and ask him to take care of this business as Tony was like a son to him. He'll be more than happy to take care of this business."

They agreed they would not tell Carol what their plan was, as it was best she didn't know.

After Carol left the club, she realized that she forgot one of Ann's drops for her ears. Ann had gotten an upper respiratory infection and even though she was over it, the doctor wanted Carol to continue the ear drops until they were gone. She had enough time to go back home, pick up the drops and get back in time for dinner with her mom and John. She hoped none of the boarders would join them as it had been quite a while since she had spent time with either of them.

She got back to her apartment in record time. Carol opened the door to the apartment and to her surprise, there was a woman wearing her robe.

"What the hell? Who are you?" Carol yelled. Eddie came out of the bedroom and was startled to see Carol.

"What are you doing here?" he asked.

"What a stupid thing to ask me. This is my apartment! The question is what she is doing here?" Carol said shaking.

Carol was in shock and full of anger and didn't wait for an answer. She pushed past Peggy, then Eddie, went to her dresser, pulled out clothes from several drawers, got a bag and stuffed whatever she could fit into the bag. She left and immediately went back to her mom's. On the way back, she was having a hard time processing what she just encountered. One of the thoughts going through her mind was a question, *was that women really wearing her nightgown? Unfortunately, the answer was in her mind as well, Yes she really was.*

Carol told her mom what happened and asked if she could stay with them for a while. John said no. He told her that she had made her bed, now she can lay in it. However, he would drive her and the baby somewhere. She took him up on the ride and ended up at Faye's house. After telling Faye what happened, Faye suggested she just move in for a while until things settle down. This became her new home for several months. As far as things settling down, they settled down alright, in divorce court.

CHAPTER 9

Murray

Carol went back to work at Behind the Scene as a floor girl and ultimately started working private parties as a server. She was still staying with Faye and they would alternate their schedules so Faye could watch Ann while Carol was working the parties.

She stopped seeing Eddie's family and the last she heard Eddie was actively deployed. What she didn't know was Bill Sullivan was no longer in business. Johnny's father saw to that. It was just chalked up to another mob killing and was never investigated.

One night while serving at a high-end party on Michigan Avenue, an older gentleman started talking to Carol. He asked her about herself and they ended up talking most of the evening. He introduced himself as Murray Altman the owner of an automotive center. He offered her a ride home, which she was grateful for. She had been taking cabs around the city and sometimes it was hard to get a cab late in the evening. They talked all through the drive and when he walked her to the door, he asked if she would like to join him for dinner sometime. Carol thought that would be nice and explained her living situation. She told him how she and her friend Faye alternate watching Ann due to their schedules. Murray suggested that he would bring dinner to her, this way neither of them had to worry about taking care of Ann. She thought that was very thoughtful and gave her more peace of mind knowing she didn't have to juggle things to have dinner with Murray.

Murray did just that the next night. Carol loved talking with him and he found her lightheartedness refreshing. Carol told him about her past and her marriage to Eddie. Murray listened and was impressed with Carol's ability to be able to let it go and move on, without any anger.

"Carol, you certainly have had a challenging life for a girl your age. So sorry that your marriage didn't work out for you and Ann," Murray said.

"Thanks, Murray. I believe you just have to keep going no matter what. Eddie was my very first love and my doorway to having a family of my own. His heavy drinking became a problem for me and yet in some odd way, I understand it. You see, when we were dating, I was much more of a free spirit. We did all sorts of things, but when I had Ann, I stopped wanting to take chances. I guess he needed more stimulation than what I was giving him. When I saw that hussy wearing my robe, I knew it was over. When something is over, it is over," Carol responded.

"Carol, you are quite a girl. I love your spunk. I would like to help you out if you'll let me. I have a friend who runs one of the departments at the newspaper and is looking for someone to do proofreading. Please let me refer you to him. I would like to see you in a more stable environment for Ann's sake."

"Oh, thank you, but I quit school so I don't have a

diploma."

"That doesn't matter. All you would do is read articles looking for any misspellings or errors. You can read, can't you?"

"Yes, of course, I can read. I also wrote for our high school paper, so I know how to write as well," Carol said smiling.

"So, you'll go to see my friend then?"

"Yes, I will go see your friend. Thanks."

Carol did go see Murray's friend at the newspaper and he hired her immediately. He also loved her positivity and lightheartedness. She now had a stable job, one that would help her financially. Carol and Murray developed a very close and deep friendship, one that evolved into a romance.

Murray is Jewish and will not marry out of his cultural religion. Yet, he has fallen madly in love with Carol, and he knows that Carol feels the same way. He definitely finds himself in emotional conflict, so he does what he can do. He got Carol and Ann their own apartment, paid the first month's rent, filled the refrigerator full of food, paid Faye for helping Carol, and bought some clothes for Ann.

Carol accepted all of it because she saw them getting married and finally she would have her family. She loved her job at the newspaper and was told eventually she would be able to move to a department where she could write articles of interest. Carol was now making enough money to pay rent and cover whatever she and Ann needed.

Carol asked Murray when they would be getting married. That was a very difficult conversation for Murray. He told her that he could never marry her because of their cultural and religious differences. In addition, it would cause real problems for him with his family. Of course, Carol felt hurt, but she continued to see him and told herself that someday he would change his mind.

❧

Things were working out fine for Carol, she even got a new babysitter for Ann. Doris lived closer to where she worked and Ann really loved her. Doris and Carol became friends and sometimes Carol would stay with Doris and have dinner instead of picking up Ann and going home. Doris loved Carol and her attitude toward life. She wished she had some of her sunny way of seeing things.

❧

One night when Murray came over Carol decided she would try one more time to talk about marriage. She made dinner and even had some Mogen David wine for him. Neither one of them drank really, but she thought she would have some wine with dinner as well. After dinner, she cleared the table, poured each one of them a little more wine and just went for it.

"Murray, let's get married. We love each other and that is all that matters." Carol said.

"Carol, we have been over and over this. Let's just be as we are and see what happens."

"No, I don't want a part-time family. I want a real family. Full time. I love you. However, I am not going to continue seeing you romantically unless you can promise that we will get married at some point."

"Sorry Carol that things have to be this way. I adore you and Ann, and will always do for you in the ways I can."

Carol poured herself another glass of wine, and said, "Murray, I think you need to leave now."

Murray got up from his chair, grabbed his hat and said, "Sorry." He then opened the door and left.

Carol sat down, and as she started to cry, she picked up the bottle of wine and drank what was left right from the bottle. She was quite a sight. Tears streaming down her face, with grape colored stains all around her mouth. Carol felt like smashing the bottle on the table, but caught herself and just hit the table with her fist. Her heart felt so heavy for she was sure that Murray was going to change his mind. But he didn't.

CHAPTER 10

Richard

Carol stopped seeing Murray and when she wasn't playing with Ann, she spent her time with Faye, Doris or at work. One day while she was doing some writing in preparation for writing articles for the paper, she thought, *it's crazy that religion separates people. It just doesn't make sense to me. So what if he is Jewish and I'm a Catholic, a divorced Catholic at that. What a title to have in this day and age. What's wrong with men these days? They all a bunch of nut cases. Maybe that should be my first article if and when I ever get a chance to get into the editorial department.*

One day after work when she went to pick up Ann from Doris' house, she saw a man in the window. She hesitated in knocking for fear she was interrupting something important or special. She finally decided she needed to get Ann so she did knock on the door. Doris was laughing as she opened the door.

"Well, come in Carol. I want you to meet someone," Doris

said. After closing the door, she went on to say, "Carol, this is my brother Richard. He's in the Air Force and just got back from the war."

"Nice to meet you Carol," Richard said.

"Nice to meet you as well," Carol responded.

"Stay for dinner?" Doris asked Carol.

"I'd love to and I'm sure Ann won't mind," Carol responded.

Ann was almost three and was getting into as much mischief as she could find. Doris had a cabinet filled with toys. Ann would sit on the floor and play with them for hours. She loves stacking the blocks, then knocking them down. Ann also liked to look at books and sometimes Doris thought that she was actually reading them. However, she knew better, even though Ann was ahead of most children her age.

❦

Richard flew 33 missions as a turret gunner in the Air Force. Although his tour was basically over, he is still on active reserve. Richard has three sisters and a brother. His brother is in the Navy and is still fighting somewhere in the Pacific. His father is an alcoholic and an abuser. He and his brother joined the armed forces to get away from all the bickering and fighting in the household. Their mother had been a professional dancer in Vaudeville. Now, she dances around flying objects thrown by her alcoholic husband. She did have another child during her Vaudevillian days but decided to give the boy to his grandparents to raise. None of the other siblings know about their half-brother at this point in time.

❧✦

Doris is engaged to a gentleman who is also in the Navy and is somewhere in the Pacific. Doris had been a model, however, that kind of work was scarce since the war began. His other sisters, Evelyn and Elaine, were married to brothers who were in the tool and die business.

❧✦

Dinner at Doris' house was a routine the following month. Sometimes when Carol got home, Murray would stop by, usually bringing something for Ann. Carol didn't mind him stopping by as she wasn't angry with him, just annoyed with his Jewish excuse. Besides, she was really enjoying Richard's company.

Richard wasn't exciting like Eddie, nor financially well off like Murray, but he was a nice, normal, stable guy, and he would make a good father for Ann. So, she said yes to Richard when he formally asked her to go out.

They spent a lot of time at the beach with Ann and sometimes one or two of his army buddies would join them. No fancy dates, just family fun. Beach days, picnics, walks, visits with his sisters, all with Ann. When Richard asked Carol to marry him, she said yes.

It was a small wedding at City Hall. Carol wasn't in love with him like she had been with Eddie, and she didn't have the deep friendship connection with him like she had with Murray, but she loved and respected Richard for the man he was. He was a good man and now she had her family. She vowed that night Ann would never come from a broken home like she did.

❧

Late one night, Richard and Carol got a very disturbing call from Carol's sister Ruth. She was crying so hard it was difficult for Carol to understand what she was saying. From what words Carol could understand she realized what Ruth was trying to tell her. William had been killed. He was fighting in Germany and became part of the battle in capturing a bridge over the Rhine. The battle has become known as the battle of Ramagen.

Carol packed a small bag and Richard picked up Ann and off they went to meet Ruth. Ruth was on her way to their mom's home. Their mom, Betty, had enough room for all of them to stay together. As soon as Ruth and Danny arrived, Richard took Danny and Ann into the parlor to play, while Carol and Betty tried to soothe Ruth.

Carol glanced in the other room at Richard and at that moment she felt a deep love for him. He was playing with Danny and Ann just like they were his own.

❧

Richard agreed to adopt Ann since Eddie had only seen Ann once since Carol left. Carol contacted Eddie through his family and he agreed to the adoption.

Carol never received child support nor did she receive any financial support from the Navy. Apparently, Eddie had been convicted of some criminal activity and spent a lot of time in Fort Leavenworth. Eddie felt relieved and readily agreed so he wouldn't have to pay all the back child support and currently wasn't in a position to pay for any future financial support.

Court proceedings went quickly and Faye and Doris

showed up in support of Richard and Carol. The judge asked Ann, who was now four years old if she would like Richard to be her daddy. She loved Richard so there was no hesitation. She made quite an impression on the judge with her grown-up articulation and he actually came down from the bench to shake her hand. Carol and Richard celebrated by taking Ann to her favorite place, an ice cream parlor. They each had chocolate sundaes with cherries on top.

CHAPTER 11

Flour Sack Heads

Things were rough for Ruth after learning of William's death. Richard had an idea that they should invest in purchasing a two flat. He felt that it was a sound financial idea, and thought it would keep the family all together. Ruth and Danny would live upstairs and Richard, Carol, and Ann would live downstairs. Their mom, Betty, was settled with John and this move would provide a new chapter in Carol's life.

Carol was always drawn back into her old neighborhoods. She loved memories and of course, Manny and the club were at the forefront of them. She would stop in just to hi to Manny and Johnny. Manny looked at her as a daughter and was always glad to see her. She brought them up to date on her marriage to Richard and the adoption of Ann. She also told him that she was going to be a homeowner and explained about purchasing a two flat with her sister on the near Northside.

"Wow, kid you've come a long way from checking hats and that loser Eddie. Let me know if you guys need anything," Manny said.

"Thanks, Manny, you have always been so good to me. You and Johnny are like family to me," Carol responded.

Carol had a stable normal life, her very own family. Ann went to a neighborhood school. Richard took the bus every morning to work and returned at night for their family dinner. Carol visited with Faye, Doris and with new friends that she had met in the neighborhood. Everyone liked Carol. She was fun and quirky, plus she had more stories than most. Then one day, everything changed.

Richard was recalled into active duty. He was to report to a base in Georgia to train troops for the Korean conflict. He left and was gone just three weeks when John died, leaving Carol's mom almost homeless. John's brother told her she could not stay in the house. Carol couldn't believe how a family could do that after all that her mom had done for John. She decided her mom would live with her and Ann.

She helped her mom pack up some things from the house and asked Murray to pick them up. While she was there, she spoke her mind to John's brother and his wife about how she felt about her mom having to leave. Carol's spunky nature showed up when she felt injustices were being committed. Although the family seemed embarrassed, that didn't change anything for Betty.

Murray was there for Carol when she needed help. He loved her and guilt was his motivator for always helping. Therefore, he said yes when Carol called and asked him if he could assist in moving her mom into their place.

It was a long day, and at the end just when the last of her mom's things were being put away, she said, "Murray would you like to stay for a cup of coffee?"

"A quick cup sounds good," Murray responded. He sat down and Carol brought him a cup. As he took it, he asked, "Are you happy Carol?"

"Yes, I am very happy. Richard is good to Ann and has provided us with a stable home. He is a very hard worker and considers Ruth and mom when making decisions that will affect our family."

"I'm glad Carol. If Richard or you need anything, let me know. Thanks for the coffee."

"Thank you for helping us. I don't think we could have gotten all of mom's things on the bus. Come by anytime."

Carol walked him to the door and felt a twinge in her heart as she closed the door behind him. Just then the phone rang.

"Hello," Carol said into the receiver.

"Hi Hon, It's me, Richard."

"Oh, so glad to hear your voice. I miss you so much!"

"Well, you won't be missing me for long. I want you to pack you and Ann up and take the bus down here and meet me. I got us an apartment off base. I'm here with a couple of my Army buddies and their wives and want you to join us. Ruth can take care of the place while we are gone."

"How exciting. I'll start packing right away. We just moved mom's things into our place. Mom is going to be staying here. John's brother wanted her to leave, so we packed her up and Murray brought everything over. This is perfect."

Murray took Carol and Ann to the bus depot downtown and helped them get settled with their luggage. Once on board, Ann settled in with the treats that Uncle Murray gave her. Her head turned every which way looking out the window as the bus rolled down the road. She loved going through the mountains on the curvy road. However, Carol wasn't as thrilled. There were times she looked out the window and couldn't see the side of the road which scared her to death.

It was the dead of the night and as black as black could be

when the bus pulled over to the side of the road. As far as Carol could tell, they still had a couple of hours to go before they arrived at their destination. The bus stopped, doors opened and two men climbed up the stairs and entered the bus. The men were wearing what looked like flour sacks on their heads. Where the traditional brand name of the flour would normally be, there were holes instead. Two holes for their eyes and one for their mouth.

The walking flour sacks approached a young Negro man and said something too low for Carol to hear. The next thing that occurred startled her. The flour sack men grabbed the man and dragged him off the bus. No one lifted a finger to help the young man. Just then Ann woke up in time to see flour heads drag the man off the bus.

Before Carol could do anything, Ann said really loud, "Mom, why were those men wearing sacks on their head? Is it Halloween here?"

Upon hearing Ann's words, the bus driver turned around and looked straight at Carol and said, "You'd better keep your little girl quiet. Let's just hope those men didn't hear her."

Carol didn't respond, but thought, *What's the big deal?*

Just then the man sitting across the aisle said, "Those men were members of the KKK, the Ku Klux Klan." At first, Carol wasn't sure if he read her thoughts or if she had said her words out loud. The man continued, "The KKK is a group of men who are filled with hatred for anyone who isn't white. Bad men who have been known to hang Negroes from trees or beat them."

Carol gasped and was glad Ann had fallen back to sleep and hoped she hadn't heard anything the man said. *What kind of situation are we going into? She thought. Hooded men who go around pulling Negro men off buses and who knows what else. I wonder what other surprises the South has in store for us.* She didn't have long to wait.

CHAPTER 12

The Dodge Takes a Nose Dive

Richard met Carol and Ann the following morning at the bus station and immediately drove them to their new home. As he drove into a rural area of Augusta, Carol told Richard about the hooded men. He assured her that she probably wouldn't encounter them again as they prefer night raids.

Low rolling hills surrounded them as they drove through blocks and blocks of row houses until they pulled up in front of one of them.

"Well, here we are, home sweet home. I thought it would be best not to live on base," Richard said. Carol agreed.

The long building had two doors at each end of the building, each representing an apartment. She followed Richard to their door and jumped when she heard hissing then saw the cage with two huge snakes in it. The cage was sitting between their door and the neighbors.

"Oh yeah, the boy next door collects snakes. The snakes are harmless," Richard said. Carol realized as she looked around their apartment that it was at the end of the row houses and bordered a wooded area.

Hooded men, snakes and now a forest. Who knows what animals live in there? This is a far cry from the city, Carol thought.

She could tell Richard arranged the furniture as it was all over the place. Carol packed up their home in Chicago and had it shipped before her and Ann left to join Richard. She sure had her work cut out for her.

Carol found it interesting that the inside walls were stucco, therefore raw and bumpy. Falling against the wall would certainly give one an interesting pattern on their body. Carol thought, *it just keeps getting better.*

That night, although she was grateful to be with Richard, she had trouble falling asleep. It was much too quiet. She was used to being lulled to sleep with the roar of busses or the rattling of trucks. She thought, *country noise is too quiet.*

Life in Georgia was moving along for Carol, Ann, and Richard. Carol did get their home in order and Ann explored the forest with the boy next door. She even helped him find snakes.

Carol met the ladies that lived in the building and some of the close row houses. They formed a very close bond and supported each other during lonely times. The neighborhood was very rural, no stores. So, the only shopping was on base at the PX or from a little bus that drove around the neighborhood and parked on a different street each day. This was so challenging for Carol being a city girl.

Instead of complaining, which wasn't her style, Carol decided to do something about this. She would learn to drive. Now that was quite the journey, however, she did get her license and then the real journey began.

One day she drove to the little bus store which was parked several blocks away, got out and forgot to put the emergency brake on. Since the neighborhood was low rolling hills, parking on a hill was the only choice. There were no sidewalks and some of the streets were lined with drainage ditches of red clay-like dirt. This was one of the streets. While she and Ann were in the little store, their car rolled down the hill, turned and ended up in the ditch, nose down.

Carol came out and just looked at the car which looked like a duck with its head buried in the sand. She thought, *well look at that. I couldn't have done that trying. This picture is worth a thousand words.*

Just then the owner of the little bus store came out and when he saw the picture that is worth a thousand words, he said, "Lady, your car is in the ditch."

Carol laughed to herself and thought, *does he think I'm blind?* Then said, "Yes, it is. I must have forgotten to put the emergency brake on. Guess it is time to get a tow truck. Do they have tow trucks around here?" she asked. But before he could answer, a tow truck appeared coming up the road.

When the truck stopped by the little bus, Carol asked the driver how was it that he came by. He told her that someone had seen her car roll into the ditch and called them. Carol didn't know who that was but was grateful for that person.

As it turned out, the car was not damaged and was drivable. Just a few scratches from the sandy clay dirt and red clay on the bumper and grill were the only tell-a-tale signs that the Dodge took a nose dive. Once all the details came out at dinner time, Richard and Carol just laughed about the incident. To Carol, what happened to the car wasn't worth getting upset over. And for Richard, he was learning to embrace Carol's lightheartedness.

CHAPTER 13

Carol the Columnist

"Hello," Carol said into the telephone receiver.

"Carol?" the voice on the other end asked.

"Yes, this is Carol. Who is this?" Carol responded.

"My name is Barbara Fuller and I am one of the editors of the paper. Your supervisor recommended you to me. I understand you traveled and met your husband who was recalled for active duty. Is this correct?" Barbara Fuller asked.

"Yes, that is correct. I am in Georgia, right outside Augusta near the base."

Barbara went on to say she would like Carol to write human interest articles about the women who joined their husbands who had been recalled to active duty for the Korean conflict. The article would come out monthly to give Carol enough time to interview women and to write the article. Carol jumped at the chance. It was agreed that Carol would send in the article one week before it was to go to print.

Carol's excitement didn't go unnoticed by Barbara who said, "You will be paid per article, plus a bonus if we get any responses from readers."

As soon as she put the phone down, she wrote a letter to Doris and to Faye about her new adventure in Georgia. She began with the men wearing flour sacks on their head, included the snakes, her learning to drive and ended with her new writing opportunity for the newspaper. She embarrassingly did put in she forgot to set the emergency brake causing the Dodge to take a dive into a ditch. She addressed the envelopes and put them on the table near the door for Richard to take in the morning.

Carol was on a mission and started talking to the ladies she met in her building to find out if they would be willing to be interviewed. Each woman eagerly wanted to share their story and how they felt being uprooted from their homes.

Carol chose a lady from a suburb of Chicago for her first article. Her name was Laura Reddy who followed her husband Roy several months ago to Georgia. Laura was a little younger than Carol with two young boys. She was a towhead blonde with a face full of freckles and had the most infectious laugh. She and Roy were one of the couples that Carol and Richard spent time with.

At first, when Laura was asked about how she felt about being "in the army" she just complained about the awful humidity and the big disgusting bugs that were everywhere. Although that was very true, Carol didn't think that is what the readers wanted to read. So, Carol went back to the drawing board and designed some questions that would lead Laura and others to dig deeper into how they were feeling about their situation.

Laura told Carol that she and her husband Roy were approved for a VA loan and had just moved into their new house. In fact, they hadn't even unpacked everything before Roy got his notification that he was being recalled to active duty. At first, she thought she would stay behind. However, Roy wanted her and the kids to join him.

Laura felt sad that she had to leave her new home, however, was happy that they were all together. Roy stayed on base sometimes and those nights were very long and lonely. Laura admitted that she started fighting depression sometime after several months of being away from home. Her friendships with the other wives have helped her with both her depression and loneliness.

Carol talked with Laura several times before writing her article. One of the emotions that Laura shared caused Carol to pause before she wrote her article. She decided that her article needed to include all of what Laura shared. Her boss could eliminate it if she felt it was inappropriate.

Laura was very bothered by the prejudice and racism in Georgia. Living just outside of Chicago, which was so diverse, she knew that prejudice existed, but never really saw it or experienced it like she is now. Two separate water fountains, two separate bathrooms, no Negroes allowed in restaurants, all of this really bothered Laura on so many levels. She felt it wasn't right that anyone had dominion over another.

It also caused problems for her with their small boys. They didn't understand when one of them was yelled at for using the wrong water fountain in a park in the city. Carol decided to include Laura's feeling about this in her article. She wrote it all in longhand and had Richard send it out. That was the beginning of Carol's writing career.

Her first article prompted so many responses from readers that Barbara was overwhelmed with all the mail coming in. She decided to forward them on to Carol. In turn, Carol read each and every one of them. They gave her not only new ideas of what kinds of questions to ask but also fueled her enthusiasm.

Each and every article Carol wrote and sent in carried some of the same challenges for the wives. Shifting of responsibilities was prominent. Women were now paying bills, negotiating with banks, paying taxes and making sure things were being taken care of back home. Another theme of the interviews was the lack of emotional support from their husbands as well as less help with raising the children. Each article prompted many responses of support from readers. Offers from readers were very generous, everything from looking after the homes they left to paying for a nanny. Many spoke to the racism as well, yet offered no solution to something that seemed too big to deal with.

The racism smacked Carol in the face one day when she and Ann went into the city to do some real shopping. She was about to enter one of the small department stores when a lady started to come out carrying quite a few boxes and bags. Carol pulled the door open and stepped back to let the lady out.

Just then another lady came up behind Carol and slapped her arm away from the door and said, "We do not hold doors for Negroes."

"Ouch, what the?" Carol said surprised by what she just encountered. Once she composed herself, she reached for the door handle once again and said, "I will hold the door for whoever I want to hold the door for. You need to step aside and let this lady through."

The lady was so stunned by Carol's brazen move, she stepped aside. I am sure she had quite the story to tell at her dinner table that night.

Carol had taken the bus into the city and when she and Ann were about to board the bus to go back home, the bus driver told her to go to the rear. Carol's skin was on the darker side due to her Native American heritage and being in the south, where it was sunny most of the time, her skin had gotten even darker. The bus driver thought she was Ann's mammy taking care of a white child. Carol nodded and she and Ann walked to the back of the bus and sat down.

When she told that story to her friends, they didn't understand why she didn't tell the bus driver she was white. Carol's response was always the same, what difference does it make what he thinks or where I sit? I now know who my next article will be about —ME!

CHAPTER 14

What's That Dangling Out the Window?

"Well Carol, I got the news today that I have been transferred to California," Richard said as he walked through the door.

"What? Come in and tell me what's going on," Carol said excitedly.

Richard sat down and told her that his unit was being transferred to California to train troops who were going to be deployed to Korea. They were to leave within the week.

Carol and Ann packed up the house, scheduled the movers and packed their Dodge coupe with what they needed for the five-day drive to California. Ann had her coloring books, crayons, and a few toys and was to share the back seat with Rex, their dog.

❧

Ruth had been watching Rex but had trouble with him, so she paid to have him flown to Georgia to be with his family. Rex was mixed with German Shepard, Spitz, and Dingo. He looked like a small German Shepard with the Spitz curly tail and the personality of a Dingo. He was an intelligent dog and very loyal to Richard. Carol was a bit scared of him because he tended to growl rather than bark, which is a trait of the Dingo. However, he was Richard's dog through and through. Richard had rescued Rex from someone who was burning him with cigarettes and kicking him. Rex was forever grateful to Richard.

One night on the road to California they stopped at a motel, as they had done the two previous nights. All the other motels they had stopped at were full. This motel had a sign that clearly stated, NO PETS. Richard's thought was to sneak Rex in since he really wasn't a barker. So, he asked Carol to tie his leash to the window handle and keep his head down while he went in to register.

Carol did, however, she forgot to roll up the window before she did so. Typical Carol. Kind of like the emergency brake situation. The minute Rex saw Richard leave the motel office and walk towards the car, he jumped out the window. However, the tied leash prevented him from reaching the ground. There Rex was dangling out the window dog paddling in the air. The motel clerk came out to see what all the commotion was about and when he saw Rex dangling, rushed over to help Richard to get him untangled before he choked to death.

Richard was embarrassed as it was obvious that they were trying to sneak Rex into the motel. The clerk felt so bad for Rex that he allowed the family to bring the dog into the motel room. That night Richard got some hamburgers for the family, and he got one for Rex too. He felt that Rex had earned it.

CHAPTER 15

Ouch, My Shoulder

California was a far cry from Georgia. Carol hated leaving Georgia and all the women she made friends with. She had grown to really like living in the South. Ann had made some really nice friends and loved playing on the tanks on the base. Carol liked watching Richard train the troops and shopping at the PX. Although she was sad to be leaving, she was looking forward to a new adventure. There will be fresh women to interview and more experiences to discover.

Richard and Carol had a difficult time finding somewhere to live within their financial budget and they weren't alone. Several of the other couples that were in Georgia with them were having the same challenge. They met and decided to drive into one of the central coastal towns and rent out a motel. There were eight couples so they thought they stood a great chance to make a deal. It worked. All eight couples got rooms and to their surprise, there were four other military couples in the motel as well. Each couple took two rooms to accommodate sleeping arrangements for their children.

A small porcelain bowl on four legs served as the sink, a four-burner miniature stove and an under the counter refrigerator were crammed in a four-foot space. A small table was next to this tiny room with two chairs.

Carol looked around and as usual, turned the situation into some humor and said, "Well, I guess I'll be making small meals and we'll just have to take turns eating."

Carol was not happy in California. She was lonely as Richard didn't come home every night. Since the base was too far to do so, he came home every four afternoons, spent the evening with Carol and Ann, then went back the next morning. The town was small with one hotel, a market, a gas station, and a long pier. Shopping was available in the next town over. However, Carol never felt comfortable driving the curvy roads along the cliffs overlooking the ocean.

The weather was getting to her as well. As she put it in letters to Ruth, Doris and Faye, *the sun doesn't come out until 11:00 in the morning and goes down by 4:00 in the afternoon. I can't wait to come home. I am really missing the city.* Carol's excitement about finally having a family of her own was waning. Feeling lonely was an all too familiar feeling to her.

Carol had already interviewed the women who were with her at the motel. There was one more woman whose husband only came home on weekends. Carol rarely saw her and was reluctant to seek her out. The unit she was in was the very last one on the end. One afternoon while Carol was sitting on her stoop with Rex, she saw the woman come out of her unit.

Carol waved, put Rex back inside and decided to walk over to her and said, "Hi, my name is Carol."

"Oh hi. I'm Mildred," she said timidly.

"How long have you and your husband been here?"

"Too long. Sorry, I'm just not in a good place. We've been here six months. Joe only comes home on the weekends and I'm about to go crazy."

"Is there anything I can do?"

"Yes, please come in for a cup of coffee for a little while."

Carol and Mildred did have that cup of coffee and the conversation became very interesting. It seems that one night someone tried to break into Mildred's unit through a window on the side, but was either unsuccessful or scared off when Mildred opened the front door to see what was going on. The person came back last night and this time Mildred actually shot at the window where she saw a shadow taking off the screen. She knew she hit him because he yelled and dropped the screen. Mildred peered out the window and saw a man running holding his shoulder.

"What? Did you tell anyone?" Carol asked.

"No, I didn't," Mildred said.

"Why didn't you call the police?"

"I was scared."

"Oh Mildred, you should tell the police. You can call them, or I will go with you to the station if you'd like."

"No, I really can't tell the police."

Carol continued trying to convince Mildred that they should go to the police. Mildred didn't want to do that for fear that Joe would be mad. He had a bad temper and she was fearful of being hit again.

"What? He hits you? Why would he be mad at you for calling the police?" Carol asked.

"Yes, he likes to use me as a punching bag when he gets home. It's like he takes his anxieties and frustration from the week out on me. He has said many times not to involve anyone in

74

our lives, that we handle our own problems."

"Well, this is your problem. He isn't here. I still think we should go to the police."

"I really want to leave Joe and go back home to Wisconsin. I can't take his temper anymore. I really think he had something to do with this."

Mildred and Carol continued to talk over coffee for quite some time. Carol was so used to asking women questions that she didn't realize she was interviewing Mildred. When she did, she said, "I'm sorry. I don't mean to be prying into your personal life."

Mildred was raised on a farm. When she was old enough, she left and moved into the city and took a job as a bookkeeper for a small company. She had a good sense of logic and a propensity for numbers. She met Joe through a mutual friend she worked with and ended up marrying him two years ago. Joe worked for a brewing company until he was recalled to active duty and sent to California.

Mildred was aware of his temper for she saw how frustrated he got when things didn't go his way, however, he never displayed any signs of physical violence. That part started shortly after they moved to California.

Carol was feeling very uncomfortable with this whole conversation. She knew she got herself into situations that were really none of her business by being nosey, as her sister always said. However, she really did believe she was there to help Mildred in some way. She decided to change the direction of the conversation until she could figure out what she should do.

Carol told Mildred that she wrote articles for a newspaper

in Chicago about military wives. She assured her that she would not write anything about Mildred. However, Mildred surprised her by saying, "Please tell my story. Maybe it can help other women who may be experiencing the same things. Besides, you have helped me and given me the strength to leave Joe. Just don't know how to do that. I don't have any money and no transportation."

Now she really was feeling uncomfortable for she was about to say something that she knew she shouldn't, but she couldn't help herself and said it anyway.

"Mildred, you don't have to worry about money for a bus ticket, I can loan it to you."

The minute those words came out of her mouth she knew she had done it again. Ruth asked her many times how does she get herself into the situations that she does. Ruth has also told her many times she gets too involved in peoples' lives, and that someday she is going to get herself in real trouble. She thought, *today just may be that day.*

"Carol, you would really do that for me? You don't even know me," Mildred said.

Carol assured her that it was okay and not to worry. She would give her money for a bus ticket and drive her to the station which was in the next town over. The town that she didn't have to drive the curvy roads along the cliffs to get there. Mildred agreed to Carol's generosity but was still worried about the man she shot.

"Well, we can't worry about that right now. How long will it take you to pack and when do you want to leave?" Carol asked.

"I've been packed for several days, since the first time that man tried to break in. Leaving is up to you. Whenever you want. The sooner the better, if that is okay with you," Mildred replied.

Carol told her that they could leave the next day and suggested she stay with her and Ann just in case the man comes back. Mildred agreed.

Ann stayed with Laura and her two boys while Carol drove Mildred to the bus station the next morning. Carol did tell Laura what was going on, just in case Richard got home early. On their drive, Carol continued questioning Mildred all the way and promised she would write her story. When they got to the bus station, Carol gave Mildred her address in Chicago since Ruth was collecting all of their mail. They hugged goodbye and Mildred climbed the stairs to the first bus she was going to be taking. Mildred felt alive and free for the first time in a very long time.

On the way back Carol wondered what happened to the man Mildred shot. She started questioning herself about not going to the police. Too late now she thought and put it out of her mind. Telling Richard was another story.

CHAPTER 16

The Price Was Right

It took a week for Mildred to make it back to her home town in Wisconsin. She went back to the farm and stayed with her parents. Mildred decided that she would help them for a while before she returned to the city to work. She needed to feel safe for the only thing keeping Joe from coming after her was the military.

Nightmares woke her up in the middle of the night. She relived all the beatings as well as the shooting. Mildred thought it best to file for divorce and knew that pretty much guaranteed Joe being deployed to Korea.

Mildred's parents couldn't believe that a perfect stranger gave her money to get back home. They were so grateful that someone reached out to their daughter that they insisted that the money be repaid right away. So Mildred mailed an envelope containing money and a letter thanking Carol for listening and for helping her. She felt so indebted to Carol and hoped someday she would be able to repay her in some way other than just returning her money.

Richard returned from the base on his usual night. While he and Carol were having dinner, she told him about meeting Mildred, the attempted break-in, the shooting and the abuse from her husband Joe. She also told him that she gave Mildred a part of their saving so she could get back home to Wisconsin.

"I can't believe how you get yourself into these crazy situations," Richard said.

"Now you sound like my sister. I was just helping someone out and yes, it is a crazy situation. Mildred had a horrible experience. She shot someone who tried to break into her unit and was scared to tell her husband. She needed a friend."

"That's why I love you so much. However, there is some truth to what your sister says. Remember when you got hit for holding the door for someone in Augusta? You do help people, and as I said, that's why I love you. However, sometimes you just charge in and don't really think of the consequences, and this time you should have gone to the police. That would have been the right thing to do." Richard responded.

"You're probably right. Well, what's done is done. Mildred is gone." Carol said.

"With Mildred gone reporting it to the police might be awkward. I think that I will come home every night this coming week just to make sure you and Ann are safe." Richard said.

"I don't think that is really necessary, but it will be nice to have you home," Carol responded.

Richard did come home the next couple of nights. Carol was happy to have her family together again, although she still didn't like the coastal town they lived in. It had been four months since they left Georgia and a year and a half since they left Chicago. Carol was very ready to get back to the windy city.

She never suspected that Ruth wanted to move or sell their building. It came as a surprise when Richard said Ruth had called him at the base informing him of that news. According to Richard she and Lester had come to that decision due to the expenses of the building. That night after dinner, Richard and Carol talked about their situation. He was not sure if he was going to be deployed to Korea and if that was the case there had to be a place for Carol and Ann to live. There was a lot to think about. The subject of Mildred and the police was put on the back burner, as one might say.

∽⁀∽

In the meantime, Paul, the man that Mildred shot, was picked up by the police in the next town over. Mildred's suspicion was right, she did hit him in his upper chest below his left shoulder. Paul didn't know what to do after he was shot. He was bleeding, in pain and knew if he went to the hospital that it would be reported to the police. So, he tried to take care of it himself. He went back to his low budget motel room and cleaned the wound. He poured himself a drink and fell asleep.

The next morning, he was burning up with fever. As he laid there, he asked himself how in the hell had he gotten himself in this position. He had met Joe at a base party. Paul had been invited as a guest of someone he knew. Joe and he started talking about business, women and the state of the nation. They really hit it off. Paul couldn't remember how the subject of killing Joe's wife came up, but somehow, he found himself agreeing to take care of the situation. Joe offered to pay him a lot of money and he just got caught up in the moment.

Paul had lost his job, his home and his wife all in the same year. Some would say Paul was a little touched in the head. So when the story came out in the newspapers no one who knew Paul was surprised. Paul thought it would be an easy deal. He blew it the first time he tried to get in the motel unit, however, the second time he tried he would have succeeded if it hadn't been that Mildred had a gun. Why didn't Joe tell him about the gun? He thought as he lay in pain.

After a couple of days of popping aspirin and throwing back shots of cheap bourbon he knew he had to go to the hospital and take his chances. Paul's life changed that day forever. The doctors did save his life. However, when he was healed enough the police came and he was taken to jail. After he told his story, Joe was picked up and charged for soliciting to murder.

Richard was on the base when the civil police came and arrested Joe, who happened to be one of the platoon leaders. Everyone watched as Joe was handcuffed and escorted into a police vehicle. Joe's temper was well known on the base and speculation was that his temper had gotten him in some sort of trouble. Little did they know they were right.

That night, Richard told Carol, he was shocked when he found out why Joe was arrested.

"Carol, you might have saved Mildred's life," Richard said.

"See, it was a good thing that I got involved. Although, I did listen to what you said the other night. I wonder what will happen to Joe."

"He will be dishonorably discharged from the service if he is convicted. It's too bad that he got himself into that fix. Well, we don't have to worry about going to the police now, for I'm sure they found him and that is what led them to Joe. It's too bad," Richard said shaking his head.

Carol did write Mildred's story about being a military wife and how it has affected her living in a remote coastal town. The article included the abuse that she endured due to her husband's stress and frustration as a platoon leader. She did not include the shooting incident nor the solicitation for murder charge that Joe was in jail for.

The month ended on a happy note. Richard was being discharged back to reserve status, as were several of the other men who had families. They stopped at the base on their way home and Carol called Ruth, Faye, and Doris and gave them all the good news. She knew they would spread the word. Richard, Carol, Ann, and Rex were on their way back home as a family. Carol was so very happy that her "tour of duty" was over.

CHAPTER 17

Read All Those Letters?

Carol loved her new apartment. It was so big and spacious. Of course, anything would be bigger than what she had lived in the last 18 months. Richard had made arrangements with Lester to find them an apartment on the north side of Chicago. He took care of all the paperwork for the rental agreement and it was ready for them and even Rex, when they returned. Life was getting back to normal. Although life with Carol was far from normal. He loved her quirkiness and her zest for life even though it got her, or both of them, into some interesting situations.

Richard started back on his job, Ann started school and Carol was still writing human interest stories for the paper. There were so many responses from the story about Mildred that her boss asked her to read all of them and respond to them by writing an article addressing their concerns. It took her quite a while to read all the letters and to pull out the main concerns and questions to speak to.

Carol let the readers know that she read every letter that came into the paper. As a result, she decided to dedicate the article to her friend and to write about spousal abuse openly.

She wrote the article by posing questions and answers she gleaned from reading all of the letters that had been sent in. Her article included some of the following:

Question: Is spousal abuse just physical or is it emotional as well? Which is worse?

Answer: Both are forms of abuse. Some of the women who responded to my original article shared that emotional abuse is actually worse than the physical. The physical pain, bruises, broken bones all eventually heal, however, the mental torment is something that never seems to go away.

Question: Why don't women leave their abusive husbands?

Answer: From the letters we received, here are some of the reasons that women don't leave. Women feel frightened about what the future will hold for them if they leave. Some feel frightened for their children or feel it is in their children's best interests to stay and keep the family together. One of the biggest reasons I read was women worried about money and their financial security if they leave.

To Carol's surprise, she was awarded the Editor's Choice Award in journalism by the three Editor- in –Chiefs from the three top newspapers in Chicago for the article she wrote on spousal abuse. She was given a plaque and taken to lunch by the Chiefs and included a surprise visit by the mayor. She was overwhelmed and couldn't believe a girl who never finished high school could ever have received such an award. Of course, she had Murray to thank for all of this.

Richard was thrilled for Carol and invited all the neighbors over for a party to celebrate Carol's success. She was so happy and proud of herself. One of the things she said to everyone that night was, "I never thought I would ever amount to anything since I was considered the "dumb one" in the family. Maybe this award will change that thought I've carried with me all my life." Everyone clapped and assured her she was far from dumb.

෭ so ৩

One day while Carol was having a cup of coffee feeling really good about herself, she received a disturbing call from Ruth. Ruth told her about the conversation she had with their mom about how she felt growing up and why she was so angry. Carol wasn't surprised that Ruth and their mom had a harsh conversation about the past. They were always arguing. It was obvious that Ruth was angry about something. She always had a chip on her shoulder and ready to pounce if someone didn't meet her expectations. That included her.

Ruth went on to tell her about the altercation she had with their dad about the same issue. Carol was a bit surprised because they always seemed to get along. Ruth was more like him and he saw Ruth as a smart businesswoman. Even though Arvin and Carol got along, he always considered her the "dumb one." He saw her as a woman who needed a man to be happy. In some ways he was right. Carol need a family, and that included a man in her eyes.

Ruth also told her how the twitching in her legs was starting to worry her as it was getting progressively worse and swore her to secrecy until she was ready to tell Lester.

While listening to Ruth, Carol thought, *I knew there was something wrong with her legs because the last time we were together I saw the top of one of her thighs continually move and bounce sporadically.* Then she remembered Ruth quickly rubbed her thigh and then stood up and changed her position before anyone else saw what was happening.

Ruth continued telling Carol she had been to many doctors and they all tell her pretty much the same thing. They feel it is caused by stress. Then she told Carol the coups de grace... the box of William's things that the military returned contained love letters to and from a French woman.

"What? I knew about the box but I didn't know about the letters. No wonder your legs twitch. I'm sure the doctors are right about it being stress. Whose legs wouldn't twitch after finding out their husband was having an affair while overseas," Carol replied.

"Carol, there's one more thing I want to tell you," Ruth said.

"What is it?" Carol asked.

"I'm sorry that I wasn't always nice to you. I realized I have not only been angry, but I've also been jealous too," Ruth said.

"Jealous? Jealous of what?" Carol asked.

"Not of what, of who. Jealous of the way you always seemed happy and loved life no matter what, and we both know our life was filled with uncertainty," Ruth explained.

Talking with Ruth that day was a very special moment in Carol's life. One that carried her through many a bad day.

CHAPTER 18

Welcome Linda Marie!

Life has a way of moving along at its own pace. Richard and Carol were waiting for their new home to be built. Carol would have liked to have things move a little faster. It seemed like a lifetime ago to Carol since they picked out their lot. And there is another thing, their names are on a doctor's list to adopt a baby. Murray and his wife just adopted a baby boy and gave Carol and Richard a lead on a doctor who may be able to help them. Carol wondered, *why is it that life moves so slow when we are waiting for something and way too fast when we are having a good time? That's a million-dollar question.*

❧

Yes, Murray stayed in Carol's life, then ultimately became part of Richards' life. He got married, although Carol nor Richard have met his wife because he keeps his friendship with them separate from his family. Richard and Murray have developed a close relationship. Murray's business is very well-known in the city. Anytime he needs help, and it's something that Richard can do, he will pay Richard on the side to work for him. The extra money really helps Carol and Richard out while they are playing financial catch up.

Richard was reluctant to have another child since Ann is a teenager now. However, Carol really wants to ensure her family will stay together and another child would give her that security. Since Carol had several miscarriages, the doctor told them that she wouldn't be able to have any more children due to some complications caused by the last one. Carol ultimately ended up with an emergency hysterectomy after she hemorrhaged one night.

Shortly after that, Carol talked Richard into adopting a baby. So with some resistance, he went with Carol to talk to the doctor referred to them by Murray. He agreed to start the application process. Carol just knew he would be just as thrilled as she was when the new baby finally arrives. She wondered which one will come first, the house or the baby. In the meantime, she cut back on her writing for the paper. It was supposed to be part-time. However, since the article on spousal abuse, more follow up articles were requested by her boss. Part-time became full-time.

Lester and Ruth moved into their new suburban home. Carol and Richard's finances did not allow them to purchase in the same development. So, they looked at model homes in the next town that was more in line with their budget. Carol was hoping that the house would be completed within the eight months that was projected. That would mean they would be in their new home for Christmas.

Danny became engaged and he and his fiancé, Bonnie, asked Ann to be in the wedding party as a bridesmaid. Ann was very excited and started going to the fittings with Bonnie. Ruth was so excited about the upcoming wedding and bought Betty a brand-new dress.

Betty quit her job at city hall after the fire. That was so scary for Ruth and Carol who were watching the building burn knowing their mom was one of the cleaning crew that was trapped in the building. She is now working at an amusement park taking tickets. Betty works during the summer and since the park closes for the winter, she is able to collect unemployment pay during the closure of the park. Carol found out that she had applied to be a foster gramma at Dunning, a mental institution. Carol just knew she would be a great foster gramma, and wished she had enough money to take care of her since she had worked so hard all her life.

🙞🙜

Even though Carol had been waiting for a call from the doctor for so long, when the phone rang, she jumped ten feet in the air. During the wait, the doctor kept them informed of the mother's pregnancy status. Carol had a feeling it was THE call and she was right.

"Hello," Carol answered.

"Is this Mrs. Adler?" The voice on the other end of the phone asked.

"Yes, who is this?" Carol asked.

"My name is Edwina and I work with Dr. Shepard. He wanted to let you and your husband know that your baby was born this afternoon. She weighs six pounds four ounces, has been checked and is in perfect health. Please come to Doctor Shepard's office tomorrow afternoon at 4:00 pm to finish signing the paperwork. He will then instruct you where and when to pick up your new baby girl. Congratulations."

"Oh my goodness. A baby girl. We will be there tomorrow for sure," Carol said. She hung the phone up and ran into the other room yelling Richard's name. "Richard, Richard.....that call was from the doctor's office. Our baby is here. She is a baby girl and we can pick her up tomorrow afternoon...or sometime tomorrow. Not sure. We just have to be at the doctor's office at 4:00 pm," Carol said all in one breath.

"What? What all did you say? Something about a baby? Slow down and tell me again," Richard requested.

After Carol caught her breath and slowly repeated what she'd said, Richard was happy because Carol was happy. He was going along with the adoption because he loved her so much. He knew how much having another child in the house meant to Carol.

⚜

The next day, Richard, Carol, and Ann went to the doctor's office, completed all the paperwork and were given directions on how to pick up the baby at the hospital. The nurse would be meeting them in the administration area in a private room. Since this was a private adoption, no one else would be involved. The name of the mother would not be known to them or anything about her.

Carol could hardly contain herself. She walked into the hospital like she was running from a bear and just started opening doors. Typical Carol behavior. There were a lot of embarrassed patients caught half-dressed or not dressed at all. Richard reached out and got a hold of Carol's arm, told her to slow down and follow him.

"Carol, I know you are excited, so am I. We have to do this the right way. Doctor Sheppard told us to go to the administration office. Even though it will be closed, he said a nurse would be waiting for us there," Richard said.

"I know. Sorry, I got carried away," Carol responded.

Carol saw the nurse and started to cry. She was holding a small bundle in her arms and walked towards Carol. She held out the baby for Carol to take. Carol reached and took the baby and said, "She feels so good in my arms."

Richard took the bag of formula and instructions from the nurse. As they walked away, the nurse said "Congratulations and good luck with your new baby girl."

Ann had been waiting in the car parked in front of the hospital. When Carol got in the front seat with her new daughter, Ann leaned over, peered down and said, "Welcome to our family." Those words "our family" brought tears to Carol's eyes.

Richard, Carol and Ann had a family meeting after Doctor Shepard's call and discussed how they were going to handle the new addition to their family. Ann offered to help after school the days she didn't work at the drug store. Richard said he would help after dinner. They had a plan. That meeting went much more smoothly than the meeting they had when they were coming up with names.

Ann had her ideas of names, Richard had his and Carol had hers. None of them matched. So each of them kept petitioning for the names they liked until the names were whittled down to ones that they all could agree upon. Robert, if the baby was a boy, and Linda Marie, if the baby was a girl.

As they pulled up to the house, neighbors were there to greet them. Richard and Carol had been in their new home just a little over two months. During this time, new families also moved into their new homes until the block was completely full. Their neighbors quickly became like family to them. They all helped each other, and everyone has been a part of this waiting game. In fact, everything that Carol and Richard needed for the baby came from neighbors and of course, Murray was right there with a crib for them.

Harry and Sandra were standing on their doorstep with balloons. Harry was in construction. Russell, who was in real estate, and Dee were also there holding a bag filled with bow-topped packages. Joining them was Dave, who owned a service station in town, and his wife Henrietta. Randy, who was a police officer, and his wife Martha, were standing by with gifts. Larry, who drove a truck for a cola company and his wife Marilyn joined the group, too. Everyone was holding packages, some had flowers and then there were Harry and Sandra's balloons.

Carol paraded by everyone with the little bundle of joy. It was like royalty parading through a crowd of supporters...and of course Linda Marie was the long awaited princess.

CHAPTER 19

Changes

The last several years have brought many changes to Carol and Richard's family. Linda Marie who has the most beautiful brown eyes and a smile that melts everyone's heart has brought them so much joy. Although, she has certainly changed the family dynamics. Carol would like to think that she has brought Richard and her closer together, however, that may not be the case. Sometimes she suspects that he's just going through the motions of being happy. Carol realized having another child put a strain on their relationship. Richard and Carol really don't have much time together anymore. Richard visits with the neighbors a lot more after dinner. He wants men friends to talk with, but Carol is missing all the conversations they used to have without all the interruptions. Changes!

Danny's wedding came and went. It was beautiful. The

ceremony was held in a Catholic Church downtown. His bride, Bonnie, looked like a princess walking down the aisle. It was a high mass so it was a very long service. Carol was having a hard time sitting and listening to the priest for it brought back memories of boarding school. One of those memories was not having a family, and how lonely she felt at boarding school.

Eating, dancing, and drinking was the theme for the reception at a fancy hotel in Chicago. So much fun! Carol and Richard danced and ate way too much. Carol was not much of a drinker, that was Richard's department. She noticed he was indulging in that area more than he usually does, and so was Ruth. It reminded her of how Eddie started drinking more heavily after they were married. She thought, *Hmm, what do I do to these men that they want to drink? That's another one of those million-dollar questions.*

Ruth really didn't drink much at social gatherings for she was always too busy dancing. So, when Carol saw Ruth drinking and not dancing at all, she was really concerned. Carol knew something was wrong but when she asked her about it, she said she would talk about it later. It was obvious she didn't want to talk in front of Lester or anyone else at the table.

Ruth told Carol later that her legs were twitching most of the time now and were getting weaker. Dancing was now out of the picture, professionally for sure and even now and then with the girls. Ruth was hopeful as her name was on a list at a research hospital to really find out what was going on with her legs. Carol felt so bad for her. She knew Ruth did not have an easy life. Ruth got the brunt of their mom and dad's divorce, and before that, she always had to watch Carol. Carol always knew that she resented that, and her as well.

Carol worried about Ruth and her legs, and feared there was something really wrong. Ruth told Carol she thought that her anger was causing physical problems. Carol really didn't know about such things. Lester got some tickets to see Dale Carnegie, who is a well-known speaker on self-improvement, and Carol was hoping whatever he says helps her in some way. She thought, *who knows, I may even go see him myself.*

Danny and his wife had a baby girl and named her Cynthia. So, now Linda Marie can grow up with a cousin. Carol and Richard's family were both small with just the two girls. Carol is excited by the possibility that her family will continue to grow.

Ann has grown into a beautiful young woman and is now engaged. She and her future husband, Craig, have been making plans for their wedding, even though it is quite a ways away. Carol thought she should be more exited, but the young man is controlling and seems to have a temper. Knowing Ann's personality, Carol knew she won't put up with either very long. Ann has her own mind and Carol couldn't see her being controlled, although she is worried that Ann is going to get hurt. His father is an alcoholic and his mom is dying from cancer. Ann is a caring girl and Carol is worried that she may be feeling sorry for this young man and that is why she said yes to marry him. Changes!

Carol and Ruth found out that their dad left Lori and got out of the prostitution business. He had some sort of accident that caused the loss of some of his fingers. Apparently while in the hospital, he and a nurse got chummy and he is now with her. They didn't know if he was married or not for neither one of them see him. Changes!

Carol was concerned about her mom. She knew her mom has had such a hard life and now is taking tickets at an amusement park to make ends meet. She doesn't live in the best of neighborhoods and worries about her walking to the bus stop every day. Carol still can't believe that her mom was asked to leave her home when John died. Sometimes she gets so mad when she starts thinking about that. Changes!

Carol's 18th birthday wish came true. She now has the family she always wanted, yet she realized that she is worrying a lot. She started thinking, I have a wonderful man in my life and two beautiful daughters, so what's going on with me? I worry about anything and everything. With all these changes I have become a worry wart. Man, I hate warts, and "worry warts" are the worst kind and the hardest to get rid of. No more worrying for me... changes, ugh!

CHAPTER 20

So Many Questions

Richard is questioning his marriage to Carol. He really isn't happy. He is feeling trapped for he didn't want another child, yet, he loved Carol and wanted to make her happy. Now, he is questioning his future with Carol. He realizes that he made a mistake by not "sticking to his guns" and giving in to adopting a child. He was torn, for he knew it was so important to Carol. He agrees a family is important. Carol was designing what a family should look like...for her. He felt they were a family before Linda Marie. He is also questioning his ability to be a father to Linda Marie, for she does have special needs. He was questioning his ability to make Carol happy. *If I were enough, she wouldn't have needed another child*, he thought to himself.

Richard was feeling overwhelmed with all the financial demands on him, as well. The bills that come as a homeowner have gone up faster than his income. Linda Marie needed some medical procedures that weren't completely covered by insurance. Her foot surgery was covered by insurance; however, the special shoes and all the therapy wasn't. It has left them with a lot of debt.

Murray has given Richard some extra work and offered to pay for Linda's treatment. Richard is a proud man and wouldn't hear of that. He is a man very clear in his values. Richard is one of the most responsible, honest men anyone would ever find. Carol has stopped her writing since Linda Marie entered their lives and that has also added to the financial stress. She spends most of her time visiting with the neighbors when she isn't with Linda Marie.

Richard spends his time across the street with one of the neighbors after dinner. That used to be the time that he and Carol would talk about things and make plans for the future. Now all Carol wants to talk about is Linda Marie, or which neighbor may be having an affair, or who just had a baby or who just got a divorce.

༺❧

One night after dinner he told Carol he would like to spend time alone for he wanted to talk to her about something. She immediately went into her fear and worry mode.

"Is everything okay?" she asked.

"Yes and No. More yes than no," he said

"Okay, I'll ask Sandra if she can watch Linda for a while this evening."

Carol and Sandra have become fast friends. In fact, all the neighbors at the end of their block have become closer over the years. The women get together in the mornings for coffee and catch up on the latest gossip and the men play street volleyball on the weekends together. Holiday get-togethers are usually pot-lucks, and of course, there is the traditional spring street dance for their community.

Once Linda Marie was at Sandra's, Richard and Carol sat down over a pot of coffee and started talking. Richard told her how he was feeling, leaving out the part of not wanting another child. Since Linda Marie was already here, he didn't think that would serve any purpose. Carol listened and wasn't completely surprised. They talked for more than two hours and decided on several things.

Carol decided to pick up some of the human interest stories the paper has been asking her to write. Since Linda Marie was getting older and really didn't need Carol in the evenings, she would be more available for some Richard and Carol time.

Richard offered one other solution to giving them some family time. They would go away for the two weeks he gets for vacation every year. That got Carol excited and suggested that maybe Harry and Sandra could go with as well. Carol told him how much she has been worrying about all the changes in the family and that she was feeling insecure. She told him that she had become a "worry wart" and how much she didn't like warts. He laughed at that and they both decided that she needed some "wart remover" and maybe a vacation would do the job.

CHAPTER 21

Hey, Buddy, Bring Me Another Bottle of Wine

Ann and Craig's wedding celebration was like a fairy tale and she did look like a princess. Her dress had two layers of white Chantilly lace, a full skirt, and a very long chapel train. Five bridesmaids and groomsmen, one junior bridesmaid, two flower girls, and two ring bearers, nineteen people all together walked down the aisle.

The bridesmaids were dressed in aqua sheath dresses with a wrap-around type skirt, which could be detached. The groomsmen wore white tuxedos with aqua shirts and white ties.

Ann carried the typical bouquet with yellow and aqua flowers sprinkled throughout. Yellow flowers were carried by the bridesmaids.

When everyone stood together for pictures, it looked like one of the paintings you would see in an art gallery. The colors looked like an artist's pallet of aqua, and yellow with white in between. So beautiful.

There was some drama before the wedding between Ann and one of the priests at the church where they were going to be married. Richard's religion is Lutheran, so Ann was raised in the Lutheran church. Carol taught Ann about the religion she was raised in which was Catholicism. Since Craig is Catholic and there are such strict rules of the church regarding an interreligious marriage, Ann decided she would go through the process of converting to Catholicism.

The young newly ordained priest, Father Paul, who was working with her wasn't prepared for Ann's questioning nature. The drama started when the priest described the rules of the church regarding marriage. Ann challenged them. The priest told her that if a Catholic and a non-Catholic get married in the church, they cannot get married on the inside of the rail in front of the priest. She asked if there were any exceptions to this rule, and he told her absolutely not. That is where the priest made his first mistake with Ann.

Ann suggested to the priest, if the church was paid enough money by the couple the rules would be put aside or broken. Of course, he denied that. When Ann left that session, she went to the library and made copies of several famous people that she had read about who were not Catholic but the rules had been broken or put aside for them. She even found articles about people who were Catholic, who had gotten married in the Church, divorced and remarried in the Church to someone else. Of course, these people were all very financially well off.

Ann brought those copies to her next session, showed the priest and said, "Now what do you have to say?"

With that, the young priest pounded his fist on the desk, and as he got up to walk out of the room in frustration, he yelled at her, "You will never make a good Catholic, for you ask too many questions." That's when Carol and Richard got the call.

It all worked its way out as the Monsignor of the Church finished working with Ann. He assured her that rules do get broken and put aside at times and she is quite right for questioning and not following anything or what anyone says blindly. So ended the drama of Ann and Father Paul.

＊＊＊

Manny pulled some strings, as Carol knew he would, for he loved Ann, and got a beautiful hall for the wedding. The room had crystal chandeliers and candle wall sconces all around the room. It was decorated in an old-world Tuscan style, with water fountains, and murals of Tuscan landscapes sporadically placed on the walls. All the doorways were arched and parts of the walls looked like some of the stucco had peeled away leaving only brick showing through. The room was large enough to hold the 450 people who were on the guest list and was absolutely first class.

Johnny not only arranged for all the alcohol but for the bartenders as well. Each table of 10 had several bottles of wine and formal settings. Johnny worked it so the bar was open, all alcoholic drinks would be free to the guests. His bartenders were instructed to make any drink that was requested, something that was unheard of at weddings. Johnny has always been good to Carol, and he also loves Ann.

The celebration was joyous, fun and full of excitement. As the seven-course dinner was being served, Carol wondered what the bill was going to look like. Richard and Carol never expected an evening like the one that they were experiencing. She put that thought aside and just enjoyed every part of the celebration.

When everyone left, including the new bride and groom, Richard and Craig's father met with the manager to settle the bill.

Carol was holding her breath when she saw the bill being handed to Richard and Craig's father. Richard looked at the bill and then looked back at me. He shook the owner's hand as well as Craig's father and walked over to Carol. He handed Carol the bill and when she saw PAID written across the paper, she gasped. Before she could say anything, one of the owners walked over and said, "Manny took care of everything."

Later Carol and Richard were surprised to find out that the hall was attached to a bowling alley, which they never saw. The bowling alley was a front for the Chicago Mob for money laundering and other illegal business transactions. Since Johnny's father is connected to the mob, he and Manny were able to arrange all of it for Ann and Craig. Manny and Johnny were not only good friends, they were family, a different kind, but family. Carol realized she never really appreciated that until now.

Ann and Craig got divorced two years later.

CHAPTER 22

Another Glass of Champagne, Please!

Betty has been working with a little boy named Louie as a foster gramma in a psychiatric hospital. She has been meeting with Louie for quite some time and tells him stories from her childhood in Kentucky. Louie saw his parents murdered, or killed and hasn't talked since. Momma has been working with him hoping to get him to say something.

Her stories must have done the trick, for Louie started talking one afternoon when they were visiting a pet shop. Betty told Carol that he was playing with a puppy and when they both fell backward Louie just started giggling and laughing. She said that he was holding on to that puppy with all his might and all of a sudden he said, "I love you." Those words made Betty a hero and somewhat of a celebrity with the staff at the hospital.

She genuinely loves Louie and cried when she told Carol

about the pet store and what he said. Her foster grandparenting did not go unnoticed by the hospital administrator. He shared the story with all the news agencies. One of the television channels came to the hospital to interview Betty live on their show.

Other news shows picked up Betty's story. In her humble way she just said she told Louie stories about her childhood. The hospital got so many letters from viewers and one of them was a book publisher wanting Betty to write children's books. So, she recruited Carol to help her.

Betty asked Carol if she would help her write down the stories. She would tell the story aloud and Carol would write it down. When Carol told the paper what she was doing, her editor was thrilled. In fact, they did a story on Betty and Louie. So many letters came in, and they sure came in handy when Betty's first book was published.

Ruth was now in a wheelchair. She was diagnosed with a nerve disease and received treatments to stop the progression of the disease. Carol felt so bad for her. She loved to dance and dancing professionally was her dream. She did do it for a while but had to stop when her legs became too weak.

Ruth is taking it all in stride. The family started to call her Ruth Van Gogh as she has taken up painting. Her first painting was a very large one and it hangs above the couch in the living room. Carol is very proud of her, and believes she is a real trooper.

Ruth was very touched when Betty asked her if she would

do the artwork for her books. Betty would tell her the theme of the story and Ruth would do the appropriate artwork to depict the story. The first piece of artwork she did for her mom's first book was a black snake going around a big rock. Ruth and Carol have heard that story many times. That book became the number one best-selling child's book.

After several books, her publisher arranged a major book signing event at Woodsworth Book Store downtown Chicago. The publisher advertised the event and Carol sent out invitations to the people who had sent letters to the newspaper in response to the story about Betty and Louie.

Murray was invited, although Betty really didn't care for him because he wouldn't marry her way back when. She eventually got over her snit, maybe because he helped her move. Who knows? Murray is a very important person in Carol's life and has become part of the family. Manny, Johnny and some of the workers at Behind the Scene and Barbara Fuller, one of the editors from the newspaper were part of the guest list. Of course, all of the neighbors were invited as well, along with some of the military families that Carol lived with.

ক্রু৯ট

Betty's publisher really went all out on the event. Violin music, waiters serving Champagne, strawberries and other hors d' oeuvres, all being carried on silver trays. Betty got the first glass of Champagne and within a few minutes, glasses were being raised all around the room while Lester made a toast to her success. She was beaming with pride. It was a bit overwhelming to Betty, so Carol sat with her for a while at the table where she was signing books. She couldn't believe so many people came out to celebrate with her.

Among the many people who attended, there was a man with two small children. After purchasing one of each of Momma's books, they sat down in one of the overstuffed chairs that were scattered throughout the bookstore. Before he started reading one of the books to the two small children who were with him, he just stared at Betty for a while. Once he started reading to the children, he continued until Betty was finished signing her last book. He approached the table at the end of the event, and went up to Betty and they seemed to be carrying on quite the conversation.

On the way home, Carol asked Betty about the man with the two small children. She said he was just really interested in her books for his grandchildren and wanted to know if she was going to continue writing. Somehow, Carol got the feeling there was more to the story, and wanted to know the identity of the mystery man.

CHAPTER 23

I Think I'm Smitten!

Carol was right. Betty did know the man she was talking to, although she didn't realize it until the end of the evening.

"I have been watching you for a while and you remind me of someone I used to know a long time ago. The person I knew was a girl named Betty," Michael Russell said.

"It's been a long time since I've been a girl," Betty said.

"And it's been a long time since I've been a young man. I wanted to talk with you because you have some of the same mannerisms as this girl."

"What is your name?"

"Michael Russell."

"I once worked for a Dr. Russell watching his children. Don't tell me that's you?"

"Yes, I am Dr. Russell. However, I am retired now. Do you remember me?"

"Yes, I remember. That was so long ago."

"Betty, would you be willing to meet me for a cup of coffee sometime soon? I would really like that."

"Oh, I don't know. It would be nice though. I guess it'd be alright."

"Good, can we meet sometime this week? I live just outside the city and can pick you up if you'd like."

"This week would be fine. However, it will be easier if I just meet you somewhere."

They agreed to meet at a restaurant for a cup of morning coffee.

Betty couldn't believe that Dr. Russell came to her book signing and they talked after all these years. She wondered what her life would have been like if she had flirted back with him back in those days. Time had been kind to him, for he was just as handsome as ever. Just thinking about their conversation gave her butterflies.

When Carol asked if she knew him, Betty didn't want to get into the story so she just made up something that would satisfy Carol. Betty decided she wasn't going to say anything about this to Carol or Ruth. She didn't want to share that moment with anyone. The truth of the matter was that she knew it was him the first time he came to her table and had secretly hoped that he would recognize her in some way. And he did!

Betty and Michael met at a restaurant not too far from where Betty lived. When she walked in the door, she spotted him waiting at a table and she felt a flutter in her heart. Michael stood up and greeted her, then pulled out a chair for her. They just looked at each other and laughed, for it became obvious to both of them they were feeling a little nervous.

Michael asked Betty if she and Arvin were still together. Betty told him about Arvin's prostitution business and the bootlegging business before that.

"Betty, sorry about your marriage. Did you remarry?" Michael asked.

"Yes, I married a man much older than me. He had a heart attack which caused his death. Michael, what about you?" Betty asked.

"I married a nurse that I met at the hospital sometime after you stopped watching Cora and Tommy. We ended up getting married but she and Cora did not get along. It came to my attention that she was actually being mean to both children. She was jealous of them and really wanted me to send them away to a boarding school. Needless to say, that ended the marriage."

"I had to send Carol to boarding school and that was really hard on both of us. I'm sorry about your marriage ending badly."

"Betty, I am so glad you agreed to meet me. I've always been sorry that we didn't meet when you were single. You know, I was falling in love with you when you were watching my children. I was sorry when you stopped working for me, but it was probably best for both of us back then."

Betty got a little flushed hearing that. "I really liked our talks when you came home from the hospital and I agree, it was for the best back then."

They talked for another two hours and ended up eating lunch after their several cups of morning coffee. They reminisced, laughed and shared their life's journey with each other. Michael did remarry after his failed marriage to the nurse; however, she was killed in an accident. After that, he never remarried.

"I see you lost your Kentucky accent," Michael said.

"Yes, through the years of reading and especially being with John, who was high up in the Democratic Party, and would correct me from time to time. But working with Louie and the social workers at the hospital really put me straight," Betty said.

"I kind of miss it. The way you would say certain things was sort of charming. Betty, I know that this may sound silly to you, but I am smitten with you, again."

"Oh Michael, at my age? I'm an old woman."

"Well, this old man may just be falling in love with you."

Betty agreed to see Michael again. This time she allowed him to pick her up from her apartment. They saw a lot of each other over the next several weeks.

Michael took Betty to places she only knew existed from what she read. There were dinners at exclusive supper clubs and even some nights of dancing. One night they were dining at an Italian restaurant sitting in one of the enclosed booths.

"Oh Michael, I feel like a school girl," Betty confessed.

"I feel like a schoolboy myself. Spending time with you over the past weeks has been some of my happiest times. Betty, I know that this may seem kind of forward, but would you ever consider getting married again?" Michael tentatively asked.

"I guess so if it is the right man. Although, I don't really know at my age."

"I think you are the perfect age. What do you think about marrying me?"

"You? Are you asking me?"

"Yes, but I was feeling my way through the question. I'm not good with rejection."

"Well, if you are asking me, Michael, I am saying YES!"

They each picked up their glass of wine, clinked glasses and Michael said, "to us."

CHAPTER 24

Afternoon Delight

After Betty's book signing event, Ruth was approached by an art critic, Jane Finch. She was also the owner of a well-known Chicago art gallery. She met Ruth at the book signing event and really liked all the art she did on Betty's books.

One day shortly after the book signing, Ruth had Jane over and shared all her paintings with her. They spent an entire afternoon looking through all of Ruth's paintings.

Jane was impressed and asked if Ruth would be interested in showing her art at an exhibit. After Ruth realized what Jane was asking, she absolutely agreed and was humbled that Jane found her paintings good enough to exhibit. Jane also said she would like to commission Ruth's art. But first, she offered to sponsor the art exhibit for that would give more visibility to her work.

❧❦

Richard and Carol did separate and ultimately got a divorce. It was mutual. Richard hadn't been happy for a while. He was bored and the minute they separated he started dating one of the neighbors who was also recently divorced.

As Carol put it one day at Ruth's, "I felt like I was in a soap opera. I watch them on television sometimes but never thought I would be starring in one. So embarrassing."

"Are they still dating?" Ruth asked.

"No, he didn't date her long, but long enough for us to become the topic of the neighborhood. Then her ex-husband shows up on my doorstep one day and asks me if I would like to have "sex in the afternoon." Sometimes I think all men are just nut jobs," Carol replied.

Carol and Ruth have been spending more time together these days. Carol was finishing up one of Betty's books and Ruth was finishing up the artwork.

"Ruth, have you talked to Momma lately?" Carol asked.

"Yes, usually every day or so. You do as well, don't you?" Ruth asked.

"Yes. But what I mean is, has Momma told you anything that she is doing that is new?"

"No, why?"

"Well, at Momma's book signing a man with two small children, who I supposed were his grandchildren, kept staring a Momma. He bought every one of her books and then waited until the end and went up to the table and talked to her. On the way home, I asked Momma if she knew him. She kind of brushed me off with some nonsense of him wanting to know if she was going to write any more books."

"I take it you didn't buy that answer."

"No." Although, it really is Momma' business. But you know me, I have to know what's going on."

"Yes, I know. You have gotten yourself is some pretty interesting situations because you just had to know. I am sorry about you and Richard. I thought Richard gave you the family you always wanted. Maybe the way you want a family to look doesn't exist."

"Maybe you're right, Ruth. Maybe you're right."

CHAPTER 25

Larry

One day not to long after Betty's book signing, Carol got a call from one of the girls she worked with at Behind the Scene. She hadn't talked with Donna for a couple of years and was surprised to get a call from her.

Manny had called Donna, who had recently gone through a divorce as well and thought she could help Carol in some way. Manny brought Donna up to date about what Carol was going through. Manny stayed in touch with all the people who worked for him in the early days of his legitimacy. He considered them family. Manny was Behind the Scene's "mother hen" or "father rooster" if you will.

Donna did reach out to Carol. It took some coercing, however, Carol finally accepted her invitation to go to a singles meeting with her. Donna had attended several meetings and thought Carol would enjoy meeting new people.

"Everyone that comes to the meetings has gone through a

divorce at one time or another. They are all there to meet new people and start a new chapter in their lives. Carol, I'm so glad you decided to come with me tonight," Donna said.

"I really didn't want to. I guess I have to start somewhere. I really wasn't in love with Richard when we got married, however, I grew to love him. Even though I wasn't that happy, I was not the one who ended the marriage. I thought I finally got my family by marrying Richard. Oh well, the best-laid plans....I forgot how the rest goes," Carol said.

""...of mice and men often go awry" is the rest of that saying. If my memory serves me right. It is from a Steinbeck novel. Whatever happened to that loser you were married to when you left the club?"

"Not sure what happened to him after the war. Yea, he was a real winner. To think he had the nerve to let another woman not only wear my nightgown but to have sex in our bed. Man, I sure got taken in by him. Although, I did love him. He was exciting and fun. Oh well, that was then, and this is now."

Since Donna had been to these singles meetings before she gave Carol a brief overview of what goes on. When people first come, there is mingling and conversation over soft drinks and snacks, then a brief meeting to take care of group business, ending with music and dancing.

As they walked into the meeting, Donna introduced Carol to some of the people she knew and men's heads turned to see who the new prospect was. The meeting started with a discussion around the funds for the group and the upcoming social events. When that part of the meeting adjourned, several musicians took their place at the front of the room and the dancing began.

It didn't take long for several of the men to ask Carol to dance. One of the last men that asked was Larry. She was quite surprised that he was such a good dancer as he was more the shy quiet type and didn't look like someone who could cut a rug, as one would say. She found him so interesting and really enjoyed talking with him.

Larry is an archeologist and is one of the curators at the History Museum in Chicago. He is in charge of the Mexican artifacts, primarily the Aztec, Inca, and Mayan pottery. He has been on many digs in Mexico and Carol found that so interesting. This was so far out of Carol's league of knowledge that she was mesmerized by his stories.

He was smitten and felt alive around Carol. Categorizing pottery is a one-person job and gets lonely at times. Even at digs, there isn't much talking. He loved the fact that she listened and seemed so very interested in what he did. Carol really liked him and agreed to see him away from the group. They spent many nights together just talking.

Larry loved hearing stories about Carol's adventures in the south. He read some of the articles she had written for the newspaper and realized how smart she really was. She had told him that she had been considered the dumb one in the family. He was sure that was because she had a zest for life and not for academia.

When she went back to get her high school diploma, she was offered a scholarship in journalism from the Editors Society, although she didn't follow through with it. Larry understood that Carol had creativity that came from inside of her and not from anything she had been taught in school.

After a couple of months of seeing Carol, Larry proposed and Carol accepted. They got married at city hall followed with a private family dinner at a local restaurant. He convinced her to go on a Mexican cruise for their honeymoon. She was apprehensive due to Ruth's condition. Larry reminded her that Ruth's husband Lester is very capable of helping Ruth. Carol knew it really wasn't about Ruth's condition, it was something else.

Carol knew she had been part of the cause of her divorce from Richard because she wasn't willing to do some of the things that Richard suggested. She likes staying close to home and to her family. Family is so important to Carol that she has always had some fear of losing what she had. Carol realized she did the same thing in her marriage to Eddie, stopped doing all the fun things they once did. After giving herself a good talking to she decided to change, even if it made her uncomfortable. Carol did just that and said yes to the Mexican cruise.

Early one morning, while she was waiting for Larry to join her on deck, Carol looked over the rail into the deep blue waters. While watching the waves come and go it came to her that it was like the rhythm of life. Each wave is a life experience and how some experiences are calm and some are choppy or rough. As she continued to watch the dance of the waves, she noticed how each one was a little different, yet it was a harmonious partnership with the water.

She looked out towards the horizon taking in the vastness of the ocean. As she did, she started having a conversation with herself. *So, maybe Ruth was right. Maybe I have been trying too hard to make my family look a certain way. Just like each wave has a different shape and form from the next, families come in different forms and shapes as well, yet they are all part of life's experiences, whether their calm, choppy or rough. How philosophical you've become Carol.*

Just then Larry joined her, took her hand and said, "I love you, thank you for being my wife. Let's you and I have some breakfast and talk about what we are going to do for the rest of our lives."

CHAPTER 26

We've Got Something to Tell You

Ann remarried a nice man named Jack and now has a little boy. She and her new family have a beautiful home in a northwest suburb. Both Ann and her husband are real go-getters. They both worked extra hours the first year of their marriage which afforded them their first home. They sold it after two years earning them quite a large profit. That profit paid for their new home. Ann currently is a stay at home mom to her little boy, Brian. Although, she is looking for something she can do that will stimulate her and bring in some money as well.

Ann has worked at something since she was 13 years old. During the summers she started a babysitting service for the neighborhood children every morning from 8:00 am until noon. She and her friend would collect the children and take them to the park for games, coloring, reading, and earned herself quite a little nest egg. During the winter, she worked at a local clothing store being paid in clothing, since she was underage.

Betty and Ann were very close. Growing up Ann spent many a night with Betty at her little one-room apartment and heard the stories that Betty is now writing about. Ann would visit Betty at the amusement park and take her to dinner since the park closed at 5:00 pm for two hours. They even took a trip to California together which was a memory they both cherished.

Ann put together a family gathering under the pretense of celebrating her first party in their new home. In reality, it was so Betty could share her good news. Betty told Ann about her and Michael. Ann, being the organizer, decided to have Michael come a little later and give Betty a chance to share her story before he got there.

Ruth, Lester, Danny, Bonnie and their daughter Cynthia were the first to arrive. Ann had quite a spread of appetizers for them to start with until the rest of the family arrived. Blue and yellow umbrellas decorated the yard and each table had blue and yellow tablecloths. Ann knew that blue and yellow was Betty's favorite color combination.

Jack, Ann's husband, was busy making margaritas when Carol and her new husband Larry walked in with Betty and Linda Marie. Larry was welcomed into the family with open arms, for he is a very warm, loving and kind man.

Everyone had gotten their appetizers and were enjoying their margaritas when the doorbell rang. All heads turned and eyes were scanning the yard trying to figure out who wasn't there. Carol got up, answered the door, welcomed Michael and escorted him to the yard where he took a seat next to Betty.

Larry leaned over and asked Carol who the man was. Just then Ann stood up and tapped the plastic glass, not as effective as if it were glass, so Ann also yelled, "Quiet everyone." When everyone finally stopped talking, Ann said, "We have a very special guest with us. I would like to introduce Dr. Michael Russell."

"Thank you, Ann, although I am a retired doctor," Michael said. He then stood up and helped Betty stand up. When she did, she said, "I asked Ann to plan this get together because I have a story to tell you all. After all, I've gotten pretty good at telling stories."

Carol said loudly, you certainly have and we are all very proud of you Momma."

"Thank you." Then she went on to say, "When I was just barely 18 years old, Arvin and I lived in a settlement house. I'm sure some of you don't know what that is. It was a big building with some private rooms, but mostly communal living. That is where Arvin's city dreams started. He was hired on in one of the garment factories and I registered with a domestic agency. My very first employment was watching Dr. Russell's, twins Cora and Tommy."

Betty was interrupted once again by Carol, "Momma, isn't Michael the man that you talked with at your book signing event?"

"Yes, Michael is that man," Betty responded.

"I knew it. I knew there was something you weren't saying," Carol said.

"I wasn't ready to talk about it. Actually, I didn't know where to start, and that is why Michael and I are here today," Betty said. Just then Ann asked if everyone would come in and get their food while it was hot. Questions, statements of surprise all being said at the same time while plates were being filled.

Once all were seated again outside, Michael and Betty took turns filling everyone in on their recent journey. Michael shared a little about his life since he lost track of Betty. He answered lots of questions about his work as a doctor and about his children. It was quite the luncheon and it ended with Michael saying, "I have asked Betty to marry me and she said yes."

"Oh Momma, how wonderful!" Carol shouted out.

"Where are you guys going to live?" Ruth asked.

"Betty has agreed to move in with me. I have a home in the Lincoln Park area of Chicago. I bought it after my wife was killed and have lived there alone since," Michael said

"Grandma, I think it's wonderful!" Danny chimed in. Just then Jack came outside with a couple of bottles of Champagne and said, "I think it's time for a toast to the happy couple." Champagne was poured and all glasses were raised, clinked and in unison "To the happy couple" was said by all.

Michael added, "One more toast please." All glasses were raised once again, and Michael said, "To something I have missed over all these past years. To Betty's fried chicken."

Everyone laughed, clinked their glasses and said, "To Betty's fried chicken!"

CHAPTER 27

To My Family

Carol and Ruth had decided to have lunch out after a morning of shopping for the upcoming wedding. While waiting for their lunches they started talking about their mom.

"Momma has done it again. She is quite a woman," Carol said.

"Yes, she certainly has overcome so many challenges in her life with grace and dignity," Ruth responded.

"Moving to the big city must have been a challenge for her after growing up on a farm in Kentucky. Listening to the stories of the communal living at the settlement house just made me cringe. How strong she must have been to work in their kitchen to secure a private room and then going to work. I don't think momma ever thought about it being hard. I'm sure she just did what she thought was the right thing to do," Carol said.

"Unlike dad, she took her responsibility very seriously. No matter what she made sure there was food on the table and clean clothes for us to wear. Where she got the energy to take care of us, go to work and bootleg to make dad happy, I'll never know. Although, I know you were so sad and even angry about being sent to a boarding school," Ruth responded.

"I know I was sent there to keep me safe. When dad left mom had to move, of course, and work two jobs. There was no safe place for me to live since you were working as well. I understand that now and also appreciate all the high-risk situations she worked in. Cleaning cages at the zoo, in of itself is disgusting let alone being poked or pinched by a gorilla. It could have been worse, like a tiger or lion getting loose. Cleaning offices in an old building like city hall, finding herself trapped by fire, and having to climb down a huge firefighter's ladder must have been so scary for her," Carol added.

"I know it was scary for me just watching it on the television. I remember the day mom was taking tickets at the amusement park when someone reached into the booth and tried to take her purse. Luckily a passerby saw it and yelled at the guy who then ran away. From that day forward she tied her purse to her ankle. Again, working in an environment that wasn't safe," Ruth said.

"I am so glad that momma has been happier over these past years enjoying the notoriety, first from the success in helping a young boy speak, although she was humble through all the interviews and the success of her books. She always loved telling stories to us as kids and to Louie, and now her stories are written in books for all to read. She is so very proud of both and when she is asked what she thinks about her success she always answers, "Who'd a thought it?" Carol responded.

"That was one of her favorite things to say...who'd a thought it." Just as Ruth finished her sentence, their lunch came. They thanked the waitress and they each started in on their sandwiches.

The whole family is looking forward to Michael and Betty's celebration. They are going to have a luncheon overlooking Lake Michigan at the Drake Hotel. Betty left all the details to Michael and he certainly is treating her like royalty. A swanky hotel, a beautiful menu to choose from and I'm sure he has an amazing gift for her. Betty's dress is powder blue, her favorite color, and Ruth and Carol got new dresses as well. Tommy, Michael's son is going to be the best man and Carol is going to be the maid of honor. Betty wanted both girls, but Ruth begged out saying it was too hard with the wheelchair to get around all the chairs.

Ann had a bridal shower for Betty and she had so much fun opening up her presents and some of them were very sexy nightgowns. At first, she blushed, which was very endearing, but then she started to get into the whole sexy nightgown thing. She laughed and held each one up and really was quite funny with some of her quips.

The day of the wedding arrived. The Drake went out of their way to welcome everyone with such grace giving everyone a feeling that they were going to a royal ball. They even had a red carpet rolled out just outside the door of the room so when everyone entered, they walked the "red carpet" just like celebrities. Everyone took a seat and Tommy and Carol walked to the front of the room and stood with the minister. Once everyone was seated all eyes turned to the door with loving expectation for Michael and Betty to appear. When the music started the minister gave the gesture to stand and with that the door opened and Michel and Betty entered the room.

When the minister started talking, all eyes were looking at Betty and she was just sparkling with joy. The ceremony was short but very touching. There wasn't a dry eye in the room for the minister really captured the story of Michael and Betty in his remarks. Michael kissed Betty and everyone stood up and clapped. It reminded Carol of the time Eddie kissed her in the Chinese restaurant and everyone stood up and clapped. She thought, *oh so long ago.*

During lunch, there was so much clinking on glasses that poor Betty and Michael had a hard time eating. They had to grab bites in between all the kissing, although they didn't seem to mind at all. In fact, Michael clinked on one of the glasses himself. Everyone in the room was basking in the warm loving ambiance of the dining room and enjoying the picture-perfect view of the lake. Carol looked around the room and realized how lucky she was to have such a wonderful family. A family of her own.

Manny and the rest of the Behind the Scene family were sitting at one of the tables. Carol had joined their family when she was 17 years old and they have supported her through thick and thin all these past years. Richard's brother and his wife and his sisters and their husbands were at the next table. They remained in Carol's life after the divorce and as they put it, we will always be family.

Then there was Jane Finch, the owner of the art gallery sitting with Barbara Fuller along with several of Betty's friends from her publishing company. Jane has helped the family immensely by representing Ruth as an artist. It has given her such confidence as well as giving her a purpose. Barbara encouraged Carol and gave her a chance to write. Although Murray, who was sitting next to her, actually got Carol the job. Yes, Murray was invited. He has been family to Carol from the beginning, too.

Several of the neighbors that lived near Carol and Richard when they were married were also at one of the tables. Ruth's family was sitting with Ann and her husband and Larry, Linda Marie and Carol had a table with Tommy and Cora and their families.

Friends, family...family, friends...all one and the same. As Carol looked around, she felt so blessed to have such a wonderful family ...and realized that she had her very own family all along.

CHAPTER 28

Three Women and Big City Dreams

One night at dinner Michael gave Betty a beautiful set of pearls as a wedding gift. That dinner was at the Grand Hotel on Mackinac Island where they were honeymooning. Betty said she had never seen anything like Mackinac. She had heard of this place in Michigan where there were no cars and the only way to get there was by a ferry. She couldn't believe she was actually riding in a horse-drawn carriage around the very place that she had heard stories about.

Betty loved the gardens and said they were breathtaking and reminded her of the rows and rows of beautiful flowers in Lincoln Park. She and Michael had a suite overlooking the lake and Michael brought her coffee every morning. Ruth and Carol got a kick out of Betty telling them how romantic it was.

❧❧

It's been a couple of years since Betty and Michael's wedding and all the members of the family are still talking about that day. Whenever Carol sees Manny, he always tells her that Michael and her mom have an open invitation to Behind the Scene anytime, on the house. Not sure Behind the Scene is Betty's cup of tea. Who knows, Michael may just take Manny's offer.

Johnny runs the club now. Manny has gotten older and is not walking very well these days. Johnny's father was killed and since then he has been taking care of the family and has held firm not to become part of the Outfit. Carol never did find out how he was killed, but she supposed it was a retaliation killing from the North Siders. Although the mob violence has subsided over the years, every once in a while, a dead body is found in a trunk of an abandoned car.

❧❧

Ruth is still painting for Jane's art gallery, even though other galleries also want to commission her art, she stays loyal to Jane. The last painting she created was so beautiful. She painted the shoreline of Chicago with Lake Michigan and Lake Shore Drive in the forefront with some of the downtown buildings in the background. She painted it in different shades of black, gray and white. Ruth said she got the idea to paint something from a photo and it really turned out well. So well, in fact, that one of the top art critics saw it at the gallery and wrote an article about Ruth in one of the major papers in Chicago.

The article prompted so much traffic for Jane that she had to hire extra help to help host visitors through the gallery, almost like museum docents. Ruth ended up spending a lot of time at the gallery answering questions about herself and her art. Lester was so in love with Ruth and so proud of her that some days he would just sit and watch her interact with people.

Ruth has become so well-known as an artist that she was invited to a luncheon hosted by several Chicago art critics at a downtown hotel. It actually turned out to be an awards ceremony for several artists. When Ruth's name was called to come forward, Lester said she almost jumped out of the chair. For a moment, he thought she was actually going to run up to the podium. However, he put his hand on her shoulder and wheeled her between the tables to the front, where she was awarded the Artists Critic Award from the City of Chicago. The award was an antique gold trophy of an artist's pallet with two paint brushes coming through the center and paint tubes behind the pallet, with her name engraved on the plate below. This had been a total surprise to Ruth.

Of course, the family's "event planner", Ann, had a celebration party at her and Jack's home for Ruth with the whole family in attendance. Ann had hand painted little ceramic art pallets for everyone. The table was set with different colored place settings with the little ceramic art pallet placed in front of each setting. Ann had also painted the centerpiece which was a ceramic jar of paint that held different colored fresh carnations. To top everything off, Ann served the most delicious roast with all the trimmings. Everyone was proud of Ruth and equally proud of Ann who not only is talented, but has such a big heart as well.

Betty started on another book at the request of her

publisher. So, Carol has been spending time helping her write the story and Ruth is creating the artwork. They don't think that their mom will ever run out of stories. If she does, her publisher will be very disappointed.

Linda Marie turned out to be a beautiful girl. She has the biggest brown eyes that one could just get lost in. Linda Marie is a very contemplative child much more serene than Ann. Carol is so happy that the two of them are good friends, even though there is such an age gap. Linda spends a lot of time with Ann and stays with her and Jack quite often. She loves Brian and gives him a lot of attention, and Ann appreciates having Linda around to help out. Ann and Jack always include Linda in most things they do, including going with them on vacations. Carol felt so blessed to have two beautiful, loving daughters and an adorable smart grandson.

Carol still sees Richard's sisters from time to time and they talk about old times. Richard remarried and lives out of state. Ann and Linda Marie talk to him every so often. However, he is married to a very controlling woman, who doesn't like to share him with the girls. She tries to convince him that since he adopted both girls that they are not really his. Doris told Carol that she set her straight in no uncertain terms. Carol just shook her head and said, "I don't understand some people, well, sometimes I don't even understand myself, or why I do certain things. I guess we all do the best we can."

Some of Carol's neighbors have moved away, gotten divorced or passed away. She loves her home with Larry, however, sometimes she misses the times in her old neighborhood. They were family. They ate together, played together, shared each other's joys and helped each other through the rough times. Time does march on and stands still for no one.

෯෧

Carol still goes into the city from time to time to visit with Faye. She has remained such a good friend. Carol also sees Donna, who brought her to the singles group where she met Larry, every once in a while. If it wasn't for her Carol would not have met her wonderful husband. So many people come and go in and out of our lives.

෯෧

Carol misses her friend, Murray, for he passed away shortly after Betty's wedding. She knows that he regretted not marrying her and tried to make up for it by always being there for her and for her family. She forgave him a long time ago. However, she wondered if he ever forgave himself.

෯෧

Barbara asked Carol if she was up to writing a human-interest story about women. Women were starting to go through the second phase of feminism and Barbara wanted to catch the wave of increased readership. She wanted a story about a strong woman or women who overcame difficult situations and succeeded. It was to be a featured story. Carol told her that she would be glad and honored to write about three women she knew that fit that bill. The title of Carol's story is *Three Women and Big City Dreams*.

THE END

About the Author

Joyce Bennett-Hall is an Author, Writing Coach, Life Coach, Counselor, Speaker, and an Ordained Minister. She is a warm, insightful professional who has spent over thirty-five years gathering knowledge and human data about different cultures and human behavior.

Joyce has published several books; A true story about her and her husband titled, PROVIDENCE, a self-help book titled, DELIBERATE DECISIONS. Her latest fictional work is the City Dreams Series – BETTY: A Story of Big City Dreams, RUTH: A Story of Center Stage Dreams, and CAROL: A Story of Family Dreams.

She is accredited with a BMsc (Bachelor of Metaphysial Sciences), MDiv (Master of Divinity), Certification in Alcohol/Drug Counseling and Recovery Coaching as well as an Ordained Minister.

As a Coach, Teacher and Speaker, Joyce helps people find their paths to successful living and happiness by assisting them in completing their goals and realizing their dreams. For more information visit Joyce's website - www.joycebennetthall.com

Books by
Joyce Bennett-Hall

Books written by Joyce Bennett-Hall can be found by visiting her website, JoyceBennettHall.com and include:

Providence: A Story of Hope, Love and Diversity

Deliberate Decisions: A Simple Guide for Real Success

Betty: A Story of Big City Dreams

Ruth: A Story of Center Stage Dreams

Carol: A Story of Family Dreams

Made in the
USA
Lexington, KY

54753597R00077